SPINE-CHILLERS

SCOTLAND & NORTHERN IRELAND

Edited by Jenni Bannister

First published in Great Britain in 2016 by:

YoungWriters

Remus House
Coltsfoot Drive
Peterborough
PE2 9BF
Telephone: 01733 890066
Website: www.youngwriters.co.uk
All Rights Reserved
Book Design by Ashley Janson
© Copyright Contributors 2016
SB ISBN 978-1-78624-139-9

Printed and bound in the UK by BookPrintingUK
Website: www.bookprintinguk.com

FOREWORD

Enter, Reader, if you dare...

For as long as there have been stories there have been ghost stories. Writers have been trying scare their readers for centuries using just the power of their imagination. For Young Writers' latest competition Spine-Chillers we asked students to come up with their own spooky tales, but with the tricky twist of using just 100 words!

They rose to the challenge magnificently and this resulting collection of haunting tales will certainly give you the creeps! From friendly ghosts and Halloween adventures to the gruesome and macabre, the young writers in this anthology showcase their creative writing talents.

Here at Young Writers our aim is to encourage creativity and to inspire a love of the written word, so it's great to get such an amazing response, with some absolutely fantastic stories. We will now choose the top 5 authors across the competition, who will each win a Kindle Fire.

I'd like to congratulate all the young authors in *Spine-Chillers - Scotland & Northern Ireland* - I hope this inspires them to continue with their creative writing. And who knows, maybe we'll be seeing their names alongside Stephen King on the best seller lists in the future...

Jenni Bannister

Editorial Manager

CONTENTS

Joshua Morris (14) 1

ASHFIELD BOYS' HIGH SCHOOL, BELFAST
Jake Lewis Bishop (13) 1
Jack Briley (12) 2
Matthew Darragh (12) 2
Joshua Dillon (12) 3
Dylan Flynn (12) 3
Jordan Horrocks (12) 4
Toby King (12) 4
Owen Samuel Lee (12) 5
Caesar Radulski (12) 5
Dylan Reilly (12) 6
CJ Rowan (13) 6
Supachok Singkanjanawongsa (13) 7
Carter White (12) 7
Adam Wylie (12) 8

BALWEARIE HIGH SCHOOL, KIRKCALDY
Ellie Thomson (12) 8
Cameron Farley 9
Joe Barretto (12) 9
Kieran Docherty (12) 10
Ellie Gibson (12) 10
Findlay Ivan Cobain (12) 11
Peter Scott (12) 11
Alice Stark (12) 12
Isla Iona Carmichael (11) 12
Nathan Fimister (12) 13
Ethan Ritchie (12) 13
Yanna McNeilly (12) 14
Jay Milne (12) 14
Holly Sorrell (12) 15
Jamie Liddell (12) 15
Alex Briggs (12) 16
Abigail Parr (11) 16
Magnus Reid (12) 17
Joanna Ramzy (12) 17
Aimée McLaren (11) 18
Kelsey Johnstone (13) 18

BANGOR GRAMMAR SCHOOL, BANGOR
Flynn Mitchell (12) 19
Callum Beal (12) 19
Ethan Wetherall (12) 20
Joseph Krakowski (13) 20
Kyle Simpson (12) 21
George Patton (13) 21
Harry Gibson (12) 22
Michael James Tresidder (13) 22
Gareth Miskimmin (13) 23
Kristen Andrew McNeice (13) 23
Theo Gilmore (13) 24
Callum Culbert (13) 24
Ryan Cunningham (13) 25
Alastair Bull (12) 25
Aristotle Bassakaropoulos (12) 26
David Martin (13) 26
Ben English (12) 27
Ethan Paul Todd (13) 27
Calum Spence (13) 28
Sebastian Mark Steven Marzanati (13) 28
Andrew Gordon (12) 29
Ben Jenkins (12) 29
Jacob McCrea (12) 30
James Dunn (13) 30
Leon Moore (12) 31
Rhys Ballance (12) 31
James Bennett (13) 32
Ben Boyd 32
Patrick Boyd (12) 33
Jordan Brown (13) 33
Jonathan Cheung (12) 34
Lee Craig (13) 34
Ben Irwin (12) 35
Ewan Kennedy (13) 35
Sean Mawhinney (12) 36
Rhys Alyxander McFall (13) 36
Samuel Moore (12) 37
Niall Sabour (13) 37
Adam Smith (12) 38
Connor White (12) 38

Rory Wood (13) 39
Jack Nesbitt (13) 39
Ross Parker (13) 40
Ben Warren (13) 40
Thomas James Spence (13) 41
Charles Bell (13) 41
Dylan Mahood (13) 42
Tony McIntyre (12) 42
Conor Campbell (12) 43
Mark Carberry (13) 43
Corey Fullerton (13) 44

BEATH HIGH SCHOOL, COWDENBEATH

Jessica Aria Shand (13) 44
Cameron Keelan (13) 45
Sinead Steel (13) 45
Amy Brown (13) 46
Rachel McIntyre (13) 46
Caitlin Petrie (13) 47
Jaimee-Leigh Hodge (13) 47
Sean Thomson (13) 48
Daniel Allan (13) 48
Lee Ferguson (13) 49
Neve McAndrew (13) 49
Aaron Stenhouse (12) 50
Josh Logan (13) 50
Jack Smith (13) 51
Jodie Park (13) 51
Ellie Mudd (13) 52
Daisy Duncan (12) 52
Katie McQuillan (13) 53
Jessica Doig (13) 53
Emma Louise Keenan (13) 54
Darci Macdonald (13) 54
Aaron Pullen (12) 55
Alisha Barney (13) 55
Lewis Campbell (13) 56
Ryan Allan (13) 56
Stephanie Coll (13) 57
Ciara Dick (13) 57
Ciara Roberts (12) 58
Emily Wilson (12) 58
Greig McHugh (13) 59
Abigail Humphries (13) 59
Robyn Thomson (13) 60

BROUGHTON HIGH SCHOOL, EDINBURGH

Shannon Jackson (16) 60
Iona Mackay (15) 61

DEANS COMMUNITY HIGH SCHOOL, LIVINGSTON

Abbie Jayne Callander (13) 61
Erin Todd (13) 62
Lara Torrance (13) 62
Lucy Young (14) 63
Emma Crosbie (14) 63
Courtney Melrose (12) 64
Rachel Smith (12) 64

DRUMGLASS HIGH SCHOOL, DUNGANNON

Jessica McMullan (13) 65
Joshua-James Thompson (13) 65

DUNCLUG COLLEGE, BALLYMENA

Sophia McAdorey (12) 66
Abbie McClintock (13) 66
Trevor Carson (12) 67
Connor Swann (13) 67
Alex Dionne Kelly (13) 68
India McNiece (13) 68
Aaron Adair (13) 69
Sarah McAnally (13) 69
Adam Boyd (13) 70
Corey Steele (13) 70
Jack Luke (12) 71
John Dundee (13) 71

HERMITAGE ACADEMY, HELENSBURGH

Eva McAloon (12) 72
Emma Louise Green (12) 72
Madeline Bridget Fuller (12) 73
Jenny Guy (12) 73
Caitlyn Mia Wright (11) 74
Rowan McKay-Hubbard (12) 74
Miles Williams (11) 75
Kory Allan (12) 75
Jodie Mackay (12) 76

KILWINNING ACADEMY, KILWINNING

Drew Begley (12) 76
Eilidh Smith 77
Halle Lara Duncan (12) 77
Ellys Rae (12) 78
Jamie Begley (12) 78
Spencer McNeil (12) 79
Jack Bruce (12) 79
Jenny Craig (12) 80
Lauryn Gray (12) 80
Jack MacMillan Stevenson (11) 81
Jack Davison (12) 81
Charlie Spence (12) 82
Brandon Sutterfield (12) 82
Tegan Higgins (11) 83
Chloe Marion-Elizabeth Walker (12) ... 83
Denise Gatherer (12) 84
Emma Gillan (12) 84
Rachael McAulay (12) 85
Lauren Boyd (11) 85
Ryan Morris (12) 86
Ethan Logan (12) 86
Ellie Buchanan 87
Tegan Long (12) 87
Emily Nelson (11) 88
Taylor Ellis (12) 88

MALONE COLLEGE, BELFAST

Myles Quinn (14) 89

ST PATRICK'S ACADEMY, LISBURN

Luke Mulholland (15) 89

ST RONAN'S COLLEGE, LURGAN

Matthew McGrath (13) 90
Aimee McVeigh (14) 90
Aaron Casey (13) 91
Daire Campbell (13) 91
Sian Heaney (14) 92
Eva Callaghan 92
Arnijs Martinsons (14) 93
Eimhin Derby (14) 93
Niall McStravick (14) 94
Aaron Joseph McGibbon (14) 94

Aaron O'Hanlon (13) 95
Joseph Tony Mallon (14) 95
Zoe Traynor (14) 96
Louise McGrath (14) 96
Shanna McCord (13) 97
Josh Devlin (14) 97
Niamh Ellen McDonald (16) 98
Patrick McShane (15) 98
Meabh McStravick (13) 99
Seán Walsh (13) 99
Jack Hannon 100
Aine Lavery McKeown 100
Hugh Hannon (12) 101
Tara Harvey (13) 101
Andrea McKavanagh 102
John McAlinden (13) 102
Jamie Menary (13) 103
Katy Magennis (12) 103
Niall McCann (12) 104
Oisin Fitzpatrick (16) 104
Aleksandra Kaszewczuk (16) 105
Chelsee Moore (16) 105
Megan Gellately (14) 106
Aidan Heaney (12) 106
Braklee Iqbal (11) 107
Aidan Hughes (12) 107
Brendan Aaron Austin (12) 108
Conal McCann (11) 108
Fiontán McComb 109
Jude McConville (11) 109
Dylan Ruddy 110
Claire Connolly (14) 110
Tara Bracken (14) 111
Caoimhe Heaney 111

THE MINI SAGAS

The Hole In His Heart

Crack. I whirled round. Behind me stood a tall silhouette of a man. It stood completely still. Slowly and carefully I walked towards it. What I saw turned my blood to ice. His eyes were open wide and wild, head tilted back slightly, looking off at the sky. His mouth was formed in a manic grin. Gradually and deliberately he brought his head down and stared straight at me. 'Watch your back,' he whispered in a creepily calm voice. I wanted to bolt, but fear rooted me to the spot as I stared at the glistening hole in his chest.

Joshua Morris (14)

The Pumpkin

A blood-curdling scream came from the pumpkin patch. Tom went to investigate. Blood, there was blood everywhere. Blood all over the pumpkins' carved faces. A laugh, an evil laugh. A laugh that filled the air with terror... Suddenly, vines came from under his feet. Tom slowly backed up, whilst the pumpkin, it... it... grew arms. Arms grew as long as the stump of a tree. The pumpkin laughed, then aggressively picked up Tom and ate him whole. It strolled away waiting for its next victim to eat. Who would it be?

Jake Lewis Bishop (13)
Ashfield Boys' High School, Belfast

The End

Fumes filled the air as the car took light, the smell of burning tyres. All of a sudden, through the black smoke, a tall, large lizard appeared and let out a scream. Everyone ran while the giant lizard followed. It destroyed everything in its sight. It was coming straight for us. There was nowhere to hide, so we just kept running until we came to a river with nowhere to go. We had two options: stay and die or jump and maybe die. But it was too late. We got grabbed and eaten alive!

Jack Briley (12)
Ashfield Boys' High School, Belfast

Old Wood Forest

Lights beamed. A shriek decimated the forest peace. A shiver of fear crept through John's body. He was scared, like in horror movies, but much worse. It went silent. Not a bird nesting, nor a stream trickling. The entire forest was desolate. John lifted his chin. He saw what he thought was smoke, smoke that had many faces. He went to investigate. All John heard were men shouting and women crying out for help. Massive iron gates enclosed the old church. John managed to squeeze through a bent piece of gate, but he didn't know he would never get out.

Matthew Darragh (12)
Ashfield Boys' High School, Belfast

Spooky House

It was late at night and it wasn't bright. Fred jumped out of his car to investigate the house. It wasn't just any old house, it looked a bit suspicious. Fred lock-picked the door and fiddled his way through a path of skeleton bones. 'This is a bit scary,' whispered Fred. After he found his way out of the skeleton bones he saw a set of stairs. Upstairs he could hear noises from the bathroom. He went to investigate. The door opened. He could see a bloodthirsty ghost. He froze with fear. The ghost picked apart his little soul.

JOSHUA DILLON (12)
Ashfield Boys' High School, Belfast

The Abandoned House

One cruel, cold, horrible night, Dylan is in bed having a... nightmare! It's horrible, he is in an abandoned house. He is having fun, when suddenly he hears noises upstairs and it's glowing. He wants to investigate it, but he gets halfway upstairs when... the stairs break and he falls into the void. Dylan's terrified, he starts crying and hoping he's not going to die. All he can hear are squeals and laughter. He is panic-stricken. He is afraid someone is going to murder him!

DYLAN FLYNN (12)
Ashfield Boys' High School, Belfast

Monster House

Sam and I heard a loud scream, it was Chloe's scream. We knew right that second that the monster had got her. But wait... we turned around and saw her bolting for dear life, with the monster pursuing. We started running around the house trying to find places to hide, but it was no use, we were all going to die. Then we heard another scream. We knew Chloe was dead. Suddenly we spotted a window so we ran and just jumped out of it. Luckily it wasn't too high.

JORDAN HORROCKS (12)
Ashfield Boys' High School, Belfast

The Bottom Of The Drive

I wondered what was at the bottom of the driveway. It looked like a person but I wasn't sure. I decided to go to bed. I woke up suddenly to a loud bang downstairs. Deciding to go check it out, I went downstairs and saw that a window was slightly open and pots were on the wooden floor. Before I knew it, someone smacked me on the back of the head and pushed me to the ground. I woke up in a van chained to the roof and floor. What could I do?

TOBY KING (12)
Ashfield Boys' High School, Belfast

Masked Mountain

Burr, umm, brum, brum went the chainsaws as we fled, getting picked off one by one. I escaped my group of friends as they were being herded like sheep. I slid down the mountainside, not even daring to glance back. I discovered a white, towering cave. Not even questioning what may lurk inside, I entered... I wondered about my most likely dead friends and how a hiking trip had ended up like this! Suddenly I heard snow crunching and the growling of the chainsaws. I buried myself in the snow, but the last thing I saw was red snow.

OWEN SAMUEL LEE (12)
Ashfield Boys' High School, Belfast

Haunted Christmas

It was Christmas: snow raining, presents and Christmas dinner. All the good things, but this Christmas was not so good. I rushed out to play in the snow when I saw a mysterious, black figure by the streetlight. My friend hit me with a snowball and when I glanced back, the figure was gone. I ran home to get my Christmas dinner. After dinner I walked upstairs to play my console. As I was going upstairs I saw the figure again and fainted. When I woke up everything was destroyed...

CAESAR RADULSKI (12)
Ashfield Boys' High School, Belfast

THE MYSTERIOUS MAN IN THE WOODS

Felix was jogging in the woods when he heard an awful spine-chilling scream. He went to investigate it. What he saw next was creepy and scary. Felix was being chased by a strange and creepy creature that was part man, bird and lion. He was being hunted down into a trap set by the creature. He took a long shortcut through the woods to get ahead of him. Felix turned, panting, touching a cut on his arm and a gruesome gash on his leg. When he thought he was safe... the creature appeared and dragged him away.

DYLAN REILLY (12)
Ashfield Boys' High School, Belfast

IS THIS ACTUALLY HAPPENING?

John and his friends entered the mysterious looking house and saw only one door down the corridor. Then suddenly the door slammed behind them. John heard someone crying behind it. 'I think we should check it out,' stated John. John, without questioning, crept down the corridor looking everywhere. He entered the room. The door suddenly slammed, lights flickered, his friends screamed and then there was silence.... The door creaked open; his friends were hanging from the ceiling. Something was breathing down his neck. Then it screamed in his face and ripped the flesh off his skull.

CJ ROWAN (13)
Ashfield Boys' High School, Belfast

The House

A loud scream came from the abandoned house. John decided to investigate. He rang the doorbell, but nobody answered so he opened the door and shouted, 'Hello! Anybody there?' Still no one answered. He crept into the hallway and wandered around. All of a sudden lights started to flicker, leading him upstairs into a room full of blood and body parts. He felt a chill go down his spine. The good thing was he didn't see the huge, dark figure behind him. The bad thing is he didn't know he would never leave the house again. Well, not alive anyway...

SUPACHOK SINGKANJANAWONGSA (13)
Ashfield Boys' High School, Belfast

The Alleyway

I heard a sudden bang and the closing of a bin as I strolled down the alleyway. It sounded like something heavy had been dumped in the bin. I crept over to the bin. I felt like I needed to investigate this loud noise coming from the bin. I tiptoed over to make less noise and be quiet, just in case something happened. I saw blood, not just blood, footprints also. Frightened, I quickly glimpsed into the bin to see a body with a note saying: 'I'm watching you, you tell anyone and I'm going to kill your family!'

CARTER WHITE (12)
Ashfield Boys' High School, Belfast

The Hangman

It's petrifying staying overnight at a castle, but the fact that we were being attached takes the prize. During the sleepless night, Darren and I heard the sound of rope being cut. Then footsteps. Suddenly it appeared. It had a black bag over its head and looked like a hangman! I glimpsed back and Darren was hanging upside-down from his sleeping bag attached to the roof! I felt something around my neck and suddenly I was hoisted up to the ceiling too. That is all I can remember. All I know is Darren is dead.

Adam Wylie (12)
Ashfield Boys' High School, Belfast

The Attic

I heard booming footsteps across the old floorboards. Finally I pushed open the door. As I walked deeper into the cold room, an old china doll up on a shelf caught my eye. I pulled it down from the shelf. The look on its face sent shivers down my spine. Suddenly the door slammed shut and the china doll fell to the ground with a *smash*! Then I felt breathing that made the hairs on my neck prick up. As I fell to the ground, the doll's eyes were staring at me. It got me...

Ellie Thomson (12)
Balwearie High School, Kirkcaldy

Legends Of The Age: The Vision

It was pitch black. The floor was damp and cold, the ceiling was filled with jagged rocks. I couldn't move. Whenever I tried pain shot through my body. I then realised... I was tied up. I heard a croaky laugh as a mysterious bulky figure emerged. I heard big padded footsteps approaching. 'Hello,' said a frog-like voice. 'Traitor,' he said, making me realise Malfor's ape army had captured me. Suddenly the jagged ceiling lit up, revealing the walls of a cave. 'Cynder!' I awoke seeing sunlight and the familiar purple body of Spyro staring at me looking a bit worried.

CAMERON FARLEY
Balwearie High School, Kirkcaldy

The Scream

I was home alone in my dark empty room, only me and my cold, dusty bed. I heard a screech coming from downstairs. My heart started pumping rapidly. My face was a bright red tomato. It couldn't have been my parents, after all they were in England. I had to go and see who, or what was screaming from downstairs. I was shaking like a rattle snake, but it had to be done. I cautiously placed my foot on the step, looked down and proceeded to walk down the crooked staircase. I heard another screech. A hand touched my shoulder...

JOE BARRETTO (12)
Balwearie High School, Kirkcaldy

Trapped

I woke smelling burning of something like flesh, fresh flesh. Then screaming, lots of screaming. Suddenly it stopped. Footsteps started. They were getting louder. I rushed to my feet feeling petrified. I trembled around the room looking for a window or door. I tripped over what I thought was a stone or a bit of wood but it turned out to be a trapdoor. I tried to open it but it was locked shut. I felt trapped and scared. I heard the unlocking of a door. I ran to a dark corner and sat. Then from behind I was pulled.

KIERAN DOCHERTY (12)
Balwearie High School, Kirkcaldy

The Unknown

Cindy woke up with a fright as something touched her foot. She woke her sister. 'It's at the door,' she said. Her sister looked, there was nothing there. 'There's nothing there, what are you on about?' she asked. Cindy curled up in a ball with her pillow in fright, as her sister bravely walked over to the door. She stood there for about thirty seconds in confusion before the door slammed shut. The loud bang of the door woke up their parents. But nobody could get in or out. The girls were terrified.

ELLIE GIBSON (12)
Balwearie High School, Kirkcaldy

The Man Of Halloween!

An ear-piercing shriek woke me up. I sat upright in bed in a cold sweat. *What was that?* I thought. Ever since last Halloween I've never slept the same. Then I heard it, the same echoing footsteps as last Halloween. It was him. As the footsteps got closer I started looking for things I could defend myself with. The door opened and I heard the laughing, the dreadful laughing, getting closer and closer. Until *bang!* I woke up with a baseball bat in my hand. I was shaking. I put the bat down, trembling...

FINDLAY IVAN COBAIN (12)
Balwearie High School, Kirkcaldy

Skull Cracker

Jim was walking quickly through the haunted forest when something as cold as ice tried to crack Jim's small, thick skull. Jim ran, then he saw an abandoned wood mill. He went to the mill. A knife rocketed straight past his head. On the roof hanging there were two bloody hands. One dropped and went straight for his throat. He was being strangled, then the other hand was coming closer. It was at his feet, then it was at his chest. Jim was petrified. He was trying to get the hands off. The other hand was now inside Jim's mouth.

PETER SCOTT (12)
Balwearie High School, Kirkcaldy

The Stumble

It was getting dark. I was trying to find a hotel for the night. I walked up a dark lane. There was a light flickering at the end. Then I heard a scream. I ran as fast as I could back down the lane. Someone was behind me. I couldn't see. My glasses were steamed up. I made it to the end, but I didn't dare stop running. I stumbled, everything went blank.
I woke up in hospital, my parents on either side. Their eyes red with tears. 'You have been out for three days. Thank goodness you are back.'

ALICE STARK (12)
Balwearie High School, Kirkcaldy

The Sinking Feeling

I started sinking into the rotten leaves, trying to scream for help but it seemed my voice was nothing but a squeak. My world went black. There was nothing left, nothing at all. I could hear children screaming beneath me, I knew that my world was gone, I would never see my family again. A voice spoke. 'Your voice is gone. I don't like sound and I heard your favourite colour is black.' I was blind, speechless and terrified. What was going to happen? I felt long ragged sharp nails running down my spine. I knew I was no more.

ISLA IONA CARMICHAEL (11)
Balwearie High School, Kirkcaldy

The Facility

I stared out into the dimly lit hallway. I crept through the hallway. In the hallway there were doors and things were going on behind the doors. Screams came from them. Some had banging from behind the door and one had blue liquid oozing from underneath the door. Suddenly one door flew off its hinges and a large yellow claw wrapped around the door frame. I ran but looked back to see the claw had gone. I ran some more but then I was pulled into a vent and dragged away into darkness. All I heard was a crunch.

NATHAN FIMISTER (12)
Balwearie High School, Kirkcaldy

That Abomination

I ran into the cabin and slammed the door. I was sure it would try to break in somehow. I shivered at the very thought of that. I usually feared nothing but that thing, it scared me. I heard something come from the corner, that abomination was in the cabin with me. I started to panic that the thing was going to catch me. It wouldn't catch me off guard. I had seen the horrors it had done to my colleagues, I wasn't going to let that happen to me. But then I heard a crack and everything faded away.

ETHAN RITCHIE (12)
Balwearie High School, Kirkcaldy

HELP ME

Tiffany was walking up a long dark driveway leading up to an old abandoned house. She walked in the house and all she felt was a cold dead hand touch her shoulder. 'Argh! Get off, get off!' It was a man! Tiffany screamed.
The man said, 'Who are you? Tell me your name,' as he threw her into the snow outside. Tiffany tried to run but the tall scary man grabbed her and chucked her against the hard barbed wire fence. Tiffany screamed, 'Help me, please help!' Tiffany fell to the ground with a thump. She was dead!

YANNA MCNEILLY (12)
Balwearie High School, Kirkcaldy

THE BEAST

A mighty roar came from above. The streetlights flickered on and off. I started to run. I shivered in pure terror. Then I saw it. A ghastly beast the size of a house above me. I felt its breath heating up the dark sky around me. A plume of fire came from behind me, roasting my back. I turned to face it, against every instinct in my body. But there was nothing there. I spun back around. I sprinted forward. I heard a mighty thump behind me. I turned slowly. I stared directly at it. It was a dragon.

JAY MILNE (12)
Balwearie High School, Kirkcaldy

Blank Out

Bloodshot open eyes, drenched hair, damp grey skin. I remembered those cold hands with sharp claws piercing through my skin. I was lowered into a damp, dark, dirty tomb. I lay there, then suddenly dirt and mud were covering me from head to toe. I gasped and panicked. Sobs were drowning in my left ear. I was no longer breathing, I went into a blank mind but thoughts were juggling around my head. It brought me into deep sleep. *Bang!* I must have woken. I gasped. A truck full of dirt was now in my mouth. I was buried alive!

HOLLY SORRELL (12)
Balwearie High School, Kirkcaldy

Hide And Howl

Sid crept through the graveyard, playing hide-and-seek with his friends Tom and Alex. He hid behind an oak tree. The wind whooshed through the branches. Sid stared up at the full moon. He heard the voice of Alex. Then a shriek from Tom. Then their footsteps. Closer and louder they became. Then suddenly they were beyond him. He heard a rustle in the oak tree, a howl. Sid's heart was beating faster and faster. Another rustle, then a growl. He screamed, he ran, he tripped. He felt paws on his back. Exhilarated howls echoed. Sid was trembling.

JAMIE LIDDELL (12)
Balwearie High School, Kirkcaldy

Stay Here

Looking around. Nobody was there but the constant eye-watering shriek was still coming from the distance. 'Hello? It's okay I won't hurt you, I just want to know where I am.' All of a sudden silence drowned the land. My throat turned dry as a bone. Out of nowhere something started ferociously clawing at my ankles. 'Stop!' I screamed, but nothing was there.
I ran. Having no clue where to go I ran like there was no tomorrow. I stopped. A cold breath was on my shoulder. I turned around. 'Stay here...' a voice said. 'Stay...' I woke up.

Alex Briggs (12)
Balwearie High School, Kirkcaldy

The Black House

'Ahh!' screamed Tiff. A wet hand grabbed her. She screamed for help but nobody could hear her. The man dragged her along the wet mud to a tall black house. There was a loud creak as the door opened. Inside the house there were two big dogs. They looked at Tiff. Tiff screamed as they pounced at her. The dogs ripped at her skin. The man grabbed the dogs off her and chucked her onto the ground. Tiff was crying and screaming. 'Nobody will hear you,' said the man. 'Just let me go please. What do you want from me?'

Abigail Parr (11)
Balwearie High School, Kirkcaldy

HOME

There it was again. That cold stare behind him. Scott hated this route. He always felt like he was being watched. But he had no choice. It was this or the river. Or the five mile detour. Feeling uncomfortable, he sprinted the last fifty metres to his house and locked the door behind him. 'Mum!?' No answer. 'Probably out at a party. I'll call her and tell her I'm home.' The phone was out of charge. Scott swore. He went to get his charger from his bedroom. Suddenly, that feeling again and a cold hand on his shoulder. 'I'm home...'

MAGNUS REID (12)
Balwearie High School, Kirkcaldy

THE CREATURE OF THE NIGHT

One windy dark night Mary was walking to her friend Sarah's house when she heard footsteps crunching in the leaves behind her. At first she thought it was just an animal but, then it got closer... 'Boo!' It jumped on her. She didn't know what it was. She kicked it off and ran but it followed her all the way to Sarah's house. She slammed the door shut and panicked. Sarah looked out the window and saw the creature. It was sure to get in sooner or later. They saw the hand first... They weren't ever seen again.

JOANNA RAMZY (12)
Balwearie High School, Kirkcaldy

LOST AND NOT FOUND!

It was dark. I was lost. Alone in the forest. I wanted to call out for help but I was too scared. Someone was watching me. I could feel their eyes as I walked nervously through. The wind whistled through the trees and the bushes rattled as if wild animals rushed by. All of a sudden the thick fog crept in like millions of ghosts gathering. I could barely see. A shadow floated by. A footstep snapped a twig on the woodland ground. A dark figure came towards me. I ran frantically but fell, no hope left, it got me!

AIMÉE MCLAREN (11)
Balwearie High School, Kirkcaldy

WILL YOU SEE ME AGAIN?

I was wandering about the graveyard because I fell out with my mum. I heard noises. I shouted, 'Who's there?' No one replied. A stranger text me which said 'I see you'. I started to shake with fear. I decided to run and go home and say sorry to my mum. As I was running I tripped over. I skinned my knees. I turned around and it was a very tall dead man that had scars all over him. He grabbed me by the neck and took me away.

KELSEY JOHNSTONE (13)
Balwearie High School, Kirkcaldy

My Nightmare Or My Horrible Reality

I was running for my life. I could hardly breathe. The creature that haunted my nightmares was chasing me. 'How?' I asked myself, I had no answer.
I'll tell you how this started. I woke to the alarm and thumping coming from my closet. I knew I would regret whatever came out, but I got up. When I went to open the door it burst open. When 'it' burst out I instinctively opened my door. I ran as fast as I could downstairs. I glanced behind me and I saw it was my nightmare.

FLYNN MITCHELL (12)
Bangor Grammar School, Bangor

When The Lights Go Out

I couldn't believe my luck. I was lost! I'd found an old visitor centre. I'd have to stay there for the night. Inside the lights flickered on. The generator was on its last legs. Suddenly something moved in the dim light. 'Hello?' I called.
'Hello Duncan,' it rattled.
'How do you know my name?' I whispered.
'Never mind,' it cackled. 'You're afraid of the dark aren't you?'
Five days later Duncan Johnston was found dead, or so they thought. The creature has shown me its ways, enlightened my mind. It's quite easy... just turn... off... the lights, right now, please.

CALLUM BEAL (12)
Bangor Grammar School, Bangor

The Mirror

I woke up in the middle of the night, seeing something moving in my mirror. I got out of my bed and walked over. It was a boy. He looked like me but had cuts on his face and neck. I woke up the next morning thinking it was a dream. The next day I woke up in the night again, seeing the same boy, this time he had no cuts and looked just like me apart from the man in the background holding a knife. He grabbed the boy's shoulder and I felt a hand on my shoulder.

ETHAN WETHERALL (12)
Bangor Grammar School, Bangor

Circus Fun!

Finally! I was at the circus! Oh, to be young again! I hopped into a ride, it took you in the mouth of a giant clown. It went slow... what was about to happen was very unexpected. Round the next corner, the track ended. 'Stay calm!' I thought. I fell down the dark hole. I slowed down, until I was... flying? There was someone dressed as a clown at the bottom of the hole, *staring*. I landed, he smiled! He pulled out something, maybe a weapon? 'Congratulations! You're the thousandth visitor! Here's 5,000 tokens for some prizes.' I laughed, nervously.

JOSEPH KRAKOWSKI (13)
Bangor Grammar School, Bangor

It's Only A Game

I was having a great day on the Xbox playing with my friend Ethan. We'd just got to the end of a campaign when the doorbell loudly chimed. I hesitated and tried to ignore it when it rang again and frustratingly ruined our game. We had now lost. I threw down the controller shouting, 'This had better be important!' When I got there the doorway was empty. I ran back to continue the game and got there just as Ethan was being dragged into the TV by the zombies of Resident Evil. The game would now be to save Ethan.

KYLE SIMPSON (12)
Bangor Grammar School, Bangor

The Kitty Kat?

Leaves crunch underneath my feet as I run through the forest. I quickly glance over my shoulder and see glowing eyes staring back at me. I weave in and out of the trees trying to lose it. I stop to catch a breath. I quickly scan my surroundings only to see it staring down at me. I try to run but there's no point. Its eyes follow me everywhere. I cannot escape. It forces me up against a wall and I gaze deeply into its eyes. My muffled screams echo through the forest, as it viciously tears into my throat.

GEORGE PATTON (13)
Bangor Grammar School, Bangor

Down The Mountain

Feet pounding, heart pumping... This is what I feel as I stumble down the mountain. A rock looms up ahead; too late I realise and fall! I hit the ground with a dull thud. I twist round to see my pursuer, his eyes glowing red as he stumbles after me. Leaping up I begin to head down the mountain once more. As I pick up speed I trip a second time and begin to roll. *Bang!* I crack my head off a boulder and suddenly see stars. I suddenly hit a tree... and see red eyes - then nothing.

Harry Gibson (12)
Bangor Grammar School, Bangor

Freddy

Norm was having a normal day. His son Freddy was at school. Norm was about to have a cup of tea when he got a phone call. *Ring, ring, ring.* Norm answered. The voice was saying that Freddy was injured and in hospital. Norm was told Freddy was at the old hospital ninety miles away. When he arrived he rushed inside, searching frantically. Freddy was nowhere to be seen. Eventually Norm found Freddy. They were so pleased to see each other again. Norm lifted Freddy into his arms. As they were leaving, an eerie voice from behind them said, *'Daddy?'*

Michael James Tresidder (13)
Bangor Grammar School, Bangor

It

Jack heard the creak, he pressed on up the stairs with uncertainty in his mind. He was almost up when he heard it again. At the top of the stairs he gave an almighty scream as he saw 'It'. He sprinted for his life and 'It' gave chase. Jack picked up his bag and turned the doorknob. Hearing the satisfying click he opened the door and ran into the nearby wood. He watched as 'It' stared from the doorway with its human eyes, almost burning a hole in Jack's green skin as Jack took its unconscious three-year-son.

GARETH MISKIMMIN (13)
Bangor Grammar School, Bangor

Darnell's Night

Darnell was spooked by the bang upstairs. He was scared and couldn't budge. Whenever he moved from the sofa and towards the stairs he heard it again. Unwilling, he went upstairs to where the banging came from. He heard the bang, but louder. Darnell didn't want to enter the room. When he reached his mum's bedroom he grabbed the handle and clicked the door open. Darnell screamed with shock. He saw his mum dangling from the fan and beside her a man holding a baseball bat. His mum was covered in blood as she said very wearily, 'Run Darnell!'

KRISTEN ANDREW MCNEICE (13)
Bangor Grammar School, Bangor

Prototype

I was the first to sign up for Viertek's new lightweight armour system, designed for soldiers at war. This one was a prototype, not fully developed yet. I was very nervous but excited. They strapped some thin metal rods onto my back, arms and legs. A quiet, near silent whirring sound happened. A green camo armour was wrapped around me, it was exciting. I looked around the room only to see him, a despised person since my young days. But he was the manager of Viertek. He looked me in the eyes and mouthed, 'It will be all over soon.'

Theo Gilmore (13)
Bangor Grammar School, Bangor

The Ones Who Dwell Beneath

It was an early, quiet night as Sam rushed out the door to work. He was late and had no choice but to take the quickest route through the graveyard. A few minutes later he heard something rustling in the bushes. It was getting dark. Sam's nerves started to jangle as he had the feeling he wasn't alone. Suddenly, he felt a tight grip around his legs. To his horror two white hands with long black fingernails started pulling him into the ground. The last thing he saw was blood-red eyes burning through him, then it went black.

Callum Culbert (13)
Bangor Grammar School, Bangor

Cute Yet Deadly

I hear its blood-curdling scream from the fog. I run hoping to escape, but it finds me hiding. All is about to end...
But let's go back to where it started. I was walking home, the fog was thick. About half way home, I noticed a trailer with a sign saying 'exotic pets for sale'. I investigated the trailer. There was a woman there. I asked 'How much?'
She replied, '£30, be warned these creatures are cursed!' I ignored her and brought a cyan one. Later it attacked me, so I climbed out the window but it followed me bloodthirstily.

RYAN CUNNINGHAM (13)
Bangor Grammar School, Bangor

The Taxidermist

'The anaesthetic will be wearing off soon, go back in and give her another dose.' The lights flicker on, I wake up, my head pounding from the anaesthetic. I realise I'm in the house my friend and I were studying. As I scan the room I see stuffed bodies everywhere. I scream as my friend is one of them. A man comes down the stairs, the person doing all of this. He is the taxidermist. I struggle to get free. He runs towards me, he sticks a needle in my arm and I collapse in a hazed state. 'Sleep tight.'

ALASTAIR BULL (12)
Bangor Grammar School, Bangor

Untitled

Last night, I was looking for children. Looking for children to play with me. Just a small game. I was very hungry. I hadn't eaten for hours. My synthetic teeth needed something. They practically screamed for something, so I went to the park. I looked at my own reflection in the lake, seeing my never-ending freakish smile and my black emotionless eyes. My instincts were seized. I bit them all, one by one, little by little. It's slower with superficial teeth, yet more fun. I made them all bleed. It was actually quite funny watching them scream. It amused me.

ARISTOTLE BASSAKAROPOULOS (12)
Bangor Grammar School, Bangor

Rise Of The Royal

One windy night, I was looking for warm shelter. I had just escaped from a fire and I desperately needed help. I saw an old castle in the distance and decided to go in. The wind slammed the doors behind me. I was trapped! Nervously I explored the castle. Suddenly, a bang came from another room! I decided to see what was going on. As I entered the room I saw the tomb wasn't completely closed. I then felt a cold hand on my shoulder. Moving was impossible. I was doomed...

DAVID MARTIN (13)
Bangor Grammar School, Bangor

The Creature

I was running away from the strange creature. It was running after me trying to kill me. When I got to my house I opened the door and then went straight to the garage to get the car. I hit the button to open the garage fully. I got in my car and started driving. I didn't know where I was driving to, just as long as I was away from the creature. As I was driving I looked behind me and saw the monster's hand reaching towards my neck. Then everything went black and I heard a crash!

BEN ENGLISH (12)
Bangor Grammar School, Bangor

Fog

I was breathing hard and panting heavy. My worn and aching feet were hitting the solid ground beneath me: *thud, thud, thud*. As I dragged myself along, I unexpectedly stumbled upon a church. On the spire it had a cross... An upside down cross? A chill shot down my spine. I peered through a red-stained glass window, and quietly peeked inside. There were seven people in pure black monk-like robes including a little boy about eight. He was levitating! An evil black fog swirled around him. Suddenly his head jerked towards me! I froze, unable to look away.

ETHAN PAUL TODD (13)
Bangor Grammar School, Bangor

Canada - Cold, Creepy and Callous

Canada - the coldest place on earth! Or so it feels like in my mountain cabin. Soon I'm going to have to get more wood for the fire. Oh, great! It's dark and snowing and there's a thunderstorm, just peachy. Walking along the treacherous path I see an axe embedded in the tree. I realise there's a note under the axe. It reads: 'You shouldn't be here'. I take no notice and carry on. But there's more notes... It's getting to my head. I stop. Something whispers in my ear, 'You shouldn't be here, get out!'
'Mum is that you...?'

CALUM SPENCE (13)
Bangor Grammar School, Bangor

The Dream

I'm in bed and I'm drifting into sleep. I wake on a plane and there are terrorists pointing guns at the passengers! The man beside me tells me to unbuckle my seatbelt. When I do that he pulls me out of my seat and we run at the terrorists! We knock one out, but they shoot my friend and start shooting passengers! They get to me last and... I wake up. Later that day I'm listening to the radio on a hike in the forest. I hear a hijacked plane crash in the forest.

SEBASTIAN MARK STEVEN MARZANATI (13)
Bangor Grammar School, Bangor

Night On Wolf Mountain

My breath came out as fog. Alone, afraid, no way to get help and surrounded by wolves. Suddenly a strong and slightly ominous wind blew through. How long were they going to stay? How long until anything? I could've been with the rest of my class but because of what I'd done, I was bullied into leaving. I heard the wolves howl simultaneously. A huge shadow appeared at the foot of my tent... 'Boo!' It was those horrible bullies. They were almost worse. I shouldn't have told them about my nightmare. If I hadn't things might have been different.

Andrew Gordon (12)
Bangor Grammar School, Bangor

The Owl Man

When I turn my light out, I check in every corner of my room for monsters. The only place I don't check... is above me. This dawned on me as I stumped my toe on the bed. I looked up... above me was a man glued to the roof with his head shrivelled round the wrong way. Staring at me. I was too shocked to move. He jumped! Landing on my stomach! His mangled face an inch from mine! I bolted up! Glad it was a dream. I stumped my toe and it dawned on me... where I never search...

Ben Jenkins (12)
Bangor Grammar School, Bangor

The Surf Monster

I pick up my backpack after a great day surfing. With phone in hand I order a Hawaiian pizza. I have five minutes until it's ready! Across the bay I see the old surf hut. Time to check it out. Walking into the old surf hut there is a light. Carefully entering a room, a smell of must is in the air. I am pushed in the back. I turn around, this stone beast with blood pouring from its mouth is towering over me. It backs me into a corner, crushing me, then devours me as if I'm a marshmallow!

Jacob McCrea (12)
Bangor Grammar School, Bangor

The Demon Teacher

I was out with my friends when we strolled past an old abandoned school. We decided to enter. As we entered via the front door it creaked open. We crept down the corridors of the old deserted school as we passed the classrooms. Each one had tipped over chairs and tables with colourful drawings on the grey and white walls. I turned to my friend Brian. 'What do you think happened here?' I asked with curiosity in my voice as I tried not to cough from the dust coming off the walls. We saw a figure down the corridor...

James Dunn (13)
Bangor Grammar School, Bangor

The Fairground Horror

A massive wheel loomed in the distance. 'It must be a fairground.' I ran down to it. I started to walk around the ground then I saw a strange figure. 'Hello,' I yelled out.
This weird voice replied, 'What are you doing here?'
'I just need somewhere to stay, that's all.' Since I could only see in front of me I felt a cold hand touch my shoulder. It wasn't good. I turned around. It was a clown with knives! I ran and ran, looking for a gate. I found it but he was there! Oh no...

Leon Moore (12)
Bangor Grammar School, Bangor

The Spooky Church

As I walked down the street I heard a scream come from the church. I phoned Ewan and Patrick and said, 'Meet me at the church.'
I entered the churchyard. I walked along the rigid stones. I heard the scream again. It was close. The door creaked open, the gargoyles towering over me. I saw shadows moving then two heads rolled: Ewan and Patrick. I heard a laugh that sent shivers down my spine... *Smack!* The next thing I knew I was tied to a chair. I woke up and thought it was a dream.

Rhys Ballance (12)
Bangor Grammar School, Bangor

A Weird Night

As the dark foggy sky pelted rain on the sidewalk, John became conscious of everything that had previously happened. John jumped up slowly and painfully as he revealed a big wound on his leg. The streets were completely empty with police tape around them. A strange anomaly, he thought. Suddenly, he remembered his boxing match. He trenched through the pelting rain. His brass knuckles were still intact along with his dignity, he hoped. He straightened his arm to reveal a strange demonic scar. Then a shadow of a distorted human being awaited ahead. 'Hello?' John said. It advanced.

JAMES BENNETT (13)
Bangor Grammar School, Bangor

The Summoning

I woke up. The birds were chirping, the sun was shining and it was a beautiful day overall. But something felt wrong. It was almost too perfect. Strange screams were ever so faintly echoing throughout the house. I decided to investigate. Strange marks were carved into the cold wall, the lights were flickering and the screams were louder now. I descended down the stairs. Every step I took my footsteps were louder. In the kitchen I saw my mother and father standing, worshipping a pot with strange markings. Suddenly a bright glow blinded me. Something came out, it leaped at me...

BEN BOYD
Bangor Grammar School, Bangor

Lost

There it was. The house loomed over me, watching my every movement. I'd been here before, but of course that was with my friends. It was beginning to get darker and the mist was rolling in quickly. I opened the rusty door and stepped in. Silence. The only sound I could hear was the sound of my footsteps and my heart beating in my ears. I moved slowly as far away as possible. I ended up in the woods, not knowing where I was. I was lost.

PATRICK BOYD (12)
Bangor Grammar School, Bangor

The Man And The Music

There once was a man whose name we do not know. He was casually walking past a house that turned out to be a haunted house. The weather was fierce outside, trees blustering, drains gurgling, rain thundering down. He walked into this house using it as a shelter. He started to hear noises coming from up the stairs, and as you expected, bad idea. As he walked up the stairs he started to hear music playing on an old record! There was no one in the house, how could this music have started playing? This man, no one can find!

JORDAN BROWN (13)
Bangor Grammar School, Bangor

Monkzolla

'This is Jordan Smith reporting live from a small island just off Portrush. It's been reported that there are mysterious sightings of 'things'. We are just about to head into a temple-like building.' *Bang!* 'What's this? Run, run, run! For the viewers, there is some deformed monkey chasing us. We've just been cornered. What do you want?'
'I'm Monkzolla.'
'Okay, but what do you want?'
'I want you!'
'Run! Nooo it's got our camera man, Adam Brown. If you can still hear me get this island locked down by the army! Please, this is for your safety. Nooo! Nooo! Noooooooo...'

JONATHAN CHEUNG (12)
Bangor Grammar School, Bangor

The Deadly Dream

'Goodnight Mum,' shouted Tom as he went up to his room and slept. He woke up the next day with a slimy tentacle over his face and his bed was alive. He discovered that his legs were the tentacles but then he sank into his mattress and fell onto a solid blue platform made of card. Out of nowhere came a huge fedora that trapped him. Suddenly the floor collapsed and he was falling towards spikes sticking out from the floor, then was soon impaled on the sharp knife-like spikes.

LEE CRAIG (13)
Bangor Grammar School, Bangor

Illusion

As I ran through the foggy forest I found an abandoned house. I didn't think twice about entering the shelter. But as I entered I saw three of my friends, Joe, Percy and Adam, but there was an old man beside them. Now I was scared. The old man looked about seventy and as scared as I was I smiled at him. He gave me an evil grin back. My friends started to melt away. I ran faster than I had ever run before but he kept on appearing in places until he was right in front of me...

Ben Irwin (12)
Bangor Grammar School, Bangor

Nightmare

There I was. Standing engulfed in the fog. I didn't know where I was or how I got there. All I could see was a creepy wooden house with rusty doors and broken windows. An old man stood at the door beckoning me in with his walking stick. Curiosity overcame my nerves as I followed him into the cobwebbed house. The dimly lit corridor had hidden the man. I spun round at the sound of the creaking floorboards behind me. There he stood, gripping a silver-bladed axe above his head. Could this be the end? Down it came. *Thud!*

Ewan Kennedy (13)
Bangor Grammar School, Bangor

The Long Walk

It was a cold dark, chilly night. 'Go on a walk,' he said, 'it will be fun.' 'Thanks Grandad!'
Now I was walking through the blustering wind and blinding fog.
I had no clue where I was! I knew I was alone, but I couldn't stop thinking I was being watched.
I occasionally felt warm breath on my shoulder, but there was no one there! The thorns kept digging into my legs, one tripped me as I ran back to my grandad's ivy-smothered barn.
As I looked up there was a 'thing' staring down at me... 'H-H-Hello?'

SEAN MAWHINNEY (12)
Bangor Grammar School, Bangor

The Forest

There I was, left alone in a forest. It was cold, the wind blew, I walked down the patch then I heard, 'John!' I heard it again. I looked up and saw Linda. Beside her was that big slimy alien. She screamed louder. So I ran, climbed up the rock and tackled the alien. Then it disappeared. I got scared. I grabbed Linda and we started to run. We ran over logs and tried not to fall. As we got faster we noticed a floating sword. We got closer, we realised he was invisible...

RHYS ALYXANDER MCFALL (13)
Bangor Grammar School, Bangor

The Farm

The creak of the gate, walking through the deserted yard. I see the fog rolling in, the wind batters the tin roof as if in warning of what lies ahead. I see the crows watching my every movement in the distance like ravens of hell. As I walk into the milking parlour I hear the barks of a hell-hound whinnying for my flesh. I hear a deathly moo and a cry of terror, then I hear dripping, coincidentally like blood, then I realise it's just the milk dripping from the clusters. The flickering light shows a shadow getting closer...

SAMUEL MOORE (12)
Bangor Grammar School, Bangor

The Cabin

John went to his family's cabin for a holiday. He arrived and noticed nobody was there. He found a note on the floor that was torn, but it read: 'Run'. That's as much as he could see. John checked his phone; no signal. John saw something moving outside. He was scared to death. He got the rifle his dad kept in the cupboard. John tried to make it to the radio tower but there was a storm. He climbed the creaky, rickety ladders to find two bodies at the top being eaten away by a mysterious creature... 'Mum? Dad?...'

NIALL SABOUR (13)
Bangor Grammar School, Bangor

The Things

Hello my name is Cecil Greenwood and I'm reporting for the last time. The Things are everywhere, we can't do anything about it now. *Crash! Bang! Boom!* The weather is wild outside and the street lamps aren't on. The shadows are messing with my head, I can't see anything. I shouted, 'Help! Anyone there?' No one replied. The town is abandoned. No one near to help me, I'm trapped. Surrounded and outnumbered, no weapon. I'm dead. But then I see a knife sitting on a worktop just waiting for use. Yes, some defence. Then I realise they are watching me!

ADAM SMITH (12)
Bangor Grammar School, Bangor

Cold Blood

I laid there, my eyes open, my blood as cold as ice. The leaves of the forest floor were smothering my face. I stood up. I was like a small fish in a big pond compared to the tall trees hanging over me. I heard a rustle coming from behind me. I stood still and slowly turned my head, not wanting to see what was behind me. Nothing was there. I breathed a sigh of relief. I heard another rustle in front of me. I got extremely scared, so I jumped and looked it in the eyes. I screamed...

CONNOR WHITE (12)
Bangor Grammar School, Bangor

Delivery!

It's a dark, rainy night. Billy is at home alone playing Xbox. His dad's out shooting raccoons. Billy hears a bang on the door, he has no idea who it is. No one would come to his house in the middle of the night. They bang again and again. Then the mad man at the door comes to a window and shouts. 'I got the grub, now where's my money!' Billy goes into a dark cupboard and picks up a baseball bat ready for anything. He opens the door, swinging the bat! He's just killed a pizza delivery man.

RORY WOOD (13)
Bangor Grammar School, Bangor

The Night I'll Never Forget!

It was a cold winter's night when I was home alone. I heard a knock at my door. I got up to answer when I heard a window smash upstairs. I started to panic and sweat but I knew that wouldn't help. I sprinted for the bathroom and locked the door. As I heard someone walk past the door I quietly unlocked the door and ran upstairs into my room and grabbed my baseball bat. I crept downstairs and smashed him in the back of the head! But as he fell I realised it was my dad!

JACK NESBITT (13)
Bangor Grammar School, Bangor

Where Are You?

'Tom you can come out now, I see you,' I said, looking at the dark shadow of my friend Tom. 'I said I can see you, come out.' His small body hiding in the corner of the dark attic. 'Tom!'
'I'm not up there,' I heard a faint voice say. As I went to walk out of the room to go and find Tom I felt a strong hand come down on my shoulder. Then I heard a loud shriek of terror. It was Tom, he was upstairs. But we weren't alone.

Ross Parker (13)
Bangor Grammar School, Bangor

Dead Or Undead?

What I'm about to pen will haunt you... I was playing a football match with my friend Sean, next goal the winner. Sean struck the ball so hard that it went crashing through the window of an abandoned shack. 'I dare you to enter and get the ball,' I whispered to him. So off he went, running as fast as he could go in order to get this terrifying ordeal over with...
Sean never came back. The last thing I heard before running off in mortal terror was a shaky voice scream, 'Sean! Are you dead? Or undead? Haha!'

Ben Warren (13)
Bangor Grammar School, Bangor

The Watcher

Me and Kelly were in my room changing as she was staying at my house overnight. My room is on the ground floor and the windows were still open. Out of the corner of my eye I saw that the bushes in my front garden were rustling but it was dark out and I thought it was just a fox so I went back to Kelly. As I was moving I heard a thud outside. I looked again. The only thing I could see were two blue eyes gazing through the bush. Then, I felt his knife slice my neck.

THOMAS JAMES SPENCE (13)
Bangor Grammar School, Bangor

No One Had To Know

Thunder rumbling on a drizzly night, with blood, oozing down my back, soaked into my shirt. I stumbled into the graveyard. The footsteps creeping slowly behind me. Suddenly I tripped on a gravestone. The gravestone I had fallen upon was my own. The date of my death - today. With my vision blurry I stumbled towards the nearest source of light. I tripped, face first into the mud at the feet of my daughter. I heard voices in my head, the guilt, fear surging through my veins, yet no one had to know... no one had to know.

CHARLES BELL (13)
Bangor Grammar School, Bangor

The Nightmare

The wind is howling like a Banshee. I lie in bed feeling a deep sense of foreboding. Something dreadful is about to happen, I can sense it. Then it comes. A soft scraping along the floor, getting louder, closer, closer. I can hear its breath. I dare not open my eyes. I am frozen. Then, I can sense something above me. Beads of perspiration form on my brow. My body is covered in sweat. Swiftly, the covers are pulled off me. I open my eyes. What I see is not human as it grabs me out of the bed.

Dylan Mahood (13)
Bangor Grammar School, Bangor

Me...

I was greeted by the sight of a wide man upon entering my bedroom. He was around six foot in height. He had dark brown hair and white eyes. He wore a red suit that looked new. In his right hand, there was a silver knife coated in blood. I looked around him and saw my wife, three-year-old daughter and one-year-old son in their usual evening attire, but they were soaked in blood! I then recognised the man, and then I realised that I was looking into the mirror! It was me, a cold-blooded murderer!

Tony McIntyre (12)
Bangor Grammar School, Bangor

The Glasgow Highway

I ran and he ran. I used to love the highway in Glasgow. The trees and the fields... until this. I had been watching him for the past few weeks... and this time he saw me. He ran so I ran. We ran until we reached the hill. We couldn't fall, so I jumped. He didn't realise what was about to happen. I opened my mouth to sink my teeth into his neck. The moon dropped behind a hill and I ran away. You know what my favourite part of this life is? Sinking my teeth into an unsuspecting human.

CONOR CAMPBELL (12)
Bangor Grammar School, Bangor

What Just Happened?

David was sitting in his room. He was playing with his toy cars when his mum called him for dinner. David said that he would be down in a minute. He continued playing with his toys when he heard a bang. Next he heard a blood-curdling scream. David didn't know what to do. He ran down the spiral stairway, fearing the worst. As he reached the kitchen door, he opened it to find his mother. She was lying on the floor, dead as a stone with blood gushing from her head. David then saw the back door close.

MARK CARBERRY (13)
Bangor Grammar School, Bangor

One Of Them

It was Monday. Darren was out playing dares with his mates. He was dared to enter the creepy abandoned shack across the street. They all thought that they were brave just sitting across the street from it. But Darren had to do his dare. There he was, walking towards the door and it fell open before he could reach it. He walked in and saw bodies scattered across the floor. It creaked as he took another step and the dead bodies awoke. Darren tried to run but his leg slipped through the floorboards...! Darren was now one of them.

COREY FULLERTON (13)
Bangor Grammar School, Bangor

Praying

As I walked into the old misty church, silence was the only thing roaming and I felt a slight chill on the back of my neck as dust mites collected in my lungs. I slowly walked up to the marble alter and suddenly a candle lit. 'In the name of the Father, the Son and the Holy Spirit, amen!' I could hear the church choir singing quietly as a large brick was thrown into the stained-glass windows, shattering the bouquets and pillars. As I looked down, I saw the priest on his knees, praying, bleeding. Dead!...

JESSICA ARIA SHAND (13)
Beath High School, Cowdenbeath

100 Word Scary Story

It was the 25th June 2002 and I had just left the house to go for my friends Lee and Josh. A while later we arrived at the abandoned school. We climbed in a smashed window. As we got into the classroom, we realised there wasn't a way out. After a while of searching Josh lifted up an old desk and found a trapdoor under it. Lee was so scared, he ran and jumped down it. Lee was gone. I smashed the glass in the door to escape. Josh and I ran down the corridor different ways... Only I returned.

CAMERON KEELAN (13)
Beath High School, Cowdenbeath

Final Breath

The smoke twirls and dances as a sick dread creeps through my mind. Slowly, I back away but its grasping tendrils curl around my fingertips, imprisoning them. I pause, then try to yank my hand away, but it refuses to move. Panic begins to overwhelm me and the tendrils make it impossible to move. I'm alone and petrified. Now the smoke is moving quicker. It starts to twist around my neck. I scream but it forces its way into my nose and mouth. All I'm thinking is I can't breathe, I can't breathe, I can't breathe... So I stop trying...

SINEAD STEEL (13)
Beath High School, Cowdenbeath

The Last Tear

No idea how long I've been here. No idea where I am. There's a stabbing pain in my chest. The trees around me are still, the ground beneath me cold. The wind is hushed. I can't feel anything anymore. The pain is slowly drifting away. I always knew Father was an evil man. He always did hate me. A single tear rolls down my face. It hurts again. It seeps into the nasty gash on my cheek. This seems to disappear, it's all over now.

Amy Brown (13)
Beath High School, Cowdenbeath

Overrun

I didn't love him anymore. I realised that a while ago, but I couldn't leave him. If I left him I'd be alone, two rejects in this overrun world. He was my safety, a good luck charm. It was because of him we weren't dead. If I left him near-death experiences would become literal death. The apocalypse was upon us, hardly any of the human race still alive. I was alive but only because of him. Yet how could I keep pretending? Was it better to die than suffer? The world was crumbling around us, surely there was no hope...

Rachel McIntyre (13)
Beath High School, Cowdenbeath

Reflection

'6'3" dark hair, dark eyes, mid 40s, if seen please contact 999.'
No, not again.
I go upstairs to check on Mr Smith's children, still there, still asleep.
Knock! It comes from downstairs. I run down to lock all of the doors, locked just in time. I sit on the couch.
Knock! Again I look to my left and out of the glass doors, I see someone that matches the description. Frantically I search for the phone.
It's only when I'm looking at the door I realise he isn't outside.
'Hello...'

CAITLIN PETRIE (13)
Beath High School, Cowdenbeath

Rejection

Hannah stood at her apartment door, petrified to go in. Her knees weak, she knew what lay behind that door and it was a monster named Jack who she stupidly fell in love with.

Hannah was a very self-conscious girl, she hated everything about herself all because of Jack. The memories came flooding back when he'd call her names and that would follow up with punches and kicks and then more and more until she lay on the ground not being able to catch a breath. She was terrified but she wouldn't leave him, because being rejected terrified her more.

JAIMEE-LEIGH HODGE (13)
Beath High School, Cowdenbeath

Off The Edge

As I look down from the top of the cliff, fear shakes my body. The wind is so fierce it's almost blowing me right off the edge but I've made my decision, I close my eyes, spread out my arms and legs and begin to walk forward. 'I won't let you scare me anymore!' I cry. 'Don't do it!' a voice shouts. I open my eyes and I am right at the edge. I'm not sure what happens. It is as if my body just shuts down and I collapse into the darkness.

Sean Thomson (13)
Beath High School, Cowdenbeath

All Alone

It is a cold dark night and I have been left alone at midnight in the centre of Trafalgar Square. I'm only fifteen, and I've been kicked out of the orphanage and left on the streets. As I walk around I see many dark figures in the distance running and fighting people for no reason at all. I hide down an alleyway hoping no one will find me in the night, but how wrong am I? Two men are approaching me, drunk and with some sort of knife. I move swiftly to try to get out of their sights.

Daniel Allan (13)
Beath High School, Cowdenbeath

Home Alone

I was in my house by myself and it was really windy. I was in my room playing my PlayStation then I heard a noise that sounded like someone was in the kitchen so I went and checked. There was nobody there so I started walking up the stairs again when I thought I saw a figure walking out the bathroom but it was nothing. I went back into my room and I could hear the wind in the chimney. Suddenly there was a loud bang. I looked out my window and saw the blue bin lying on the ground.

LEE FERGUSON (13)
Beath High School, Cowdenbeath

Alcohol

The young boy cowered in the dark corner, watching as his drunk father staggered around the house, the smell of alcohol coming off of him. Tom didn't like when his father got like this. It terrified him. He got up slowly and crept over to him, trying not to anger him. He knew what happened when he did. He carefully tried to get him to sit down. His dad was trying to escape his grip, hands and legs thrashing about wildly until he got a hold of his son. His large hands gripped his neck, fist colliding with his face.

NEVE MCANDREW (13)
Beath High School, Cowdenbeath

The Ladder

I climb the rusty ladder, each step filling me with fear. I can feel my heart thumping through my ears. I dare to look down. At last I reach the top rung. I throw myself on the roof. I can see the ball, tucked in the corner. I grab it, then I throw it down. Now it's my turn. I grab the ladder and gulp.

Aaron Stenhouse (12)
Beath High School, Cowdenbeath

Fear

I dreamt I was falling off the Empire State Building in New York. I was left lying on the ground, I had only fallen from the fifteenth floor. I felt my body freeze on the ground and I lost the feeling. The last thing I remembered was lying on the ground outside with someone telling me to stay with them, but the more I tried the more tired I became until I closed my eyes and waited. My biggest fear had come true. That's when darkness invaded, shut down my body and swarmed my eyesight. I was dead...

Josh Logan (13)
Beath High School, Cowdenbeath

Them

I was lying on the cold sand, my hands covered in blood. They were looking for me. I was trying to hide from them. I wasn't going to die today. The desert was scarce, my only weapon was a rusted 44 Magnum with a few bullets left in the barrel. I was alone until suddenly I heard voices in the distance, it was them. They walked past. Out of the blue one turned around and started shooting at me, the rest did as well, their bullets hitting the golden sand *Pow!* One hit me in the foot. Death was approaching....

JACK SMITH (13)
Beath High School, Cowdenbeath

A Thousand Spiders

I was slowly walking past an eerie, creepy old house. Suddenly a dash of lightning struck the window, making it shatter into tiny little pieces, falling on the rough slabs on the floor. I turned back around and started to walk faster but then I heard a loud scattering noise. I turned back around to see what it was and all I saw was black-bodied red-eyed spiders crawling faster and faster towards me. I started yelling at the top of my voice but the spiders were covering me over my mouth, over my body. I couldn't breathe...

JODIE PARK (13)
Beath High School, Cowdenbeath

Cliff Edge

Sitting, looking, wondering whether to jump. The sea always looked better from the edge of a cliff. Ships covered by fog, moon shadowed by the clouds. Bullies forced me up here. Their words screaming over and over in my head. I could see the fog closing in, spirals twirling, forming shapes and shadows. One I recognised, followed by a voice. A family member. My mum. She was calling, telling me to stay strong. The wind then started to howl and the fog turned black. I couldn't see anything. My mum taken again. I have to jump. That's the only cure.

Ellie Mudd (13)
Beath High School, Cowdenbeath

My Fear

I never had a fear, that was until now. The past few nights there have been weird things happening. My phone's been glitching. I hear things. I see things.
That's what's been happening. For some reason the other side has always seemed appealing, I kind of like the idea of it. When watching movies I hear banging and someone whispers to me, 'That's what happens when you believe.' Opening and closing doors, lights on and off, things move. My body always feels someone's watching me. My fear? The paranormal.

Daisy Duncan (12)
Beath High School, Cowdenbeath

Overcome

I knew I had to. I had to do it. My life depended on it. I wanted to do it so badly but my brain was telling my legs no! I had to enter that lift, I had to! Shaking with fear every step I took I knew he would nearly have caught up by now. I heard the footsteps in my ringing ears, and the thumping beat of my heart through my ponytail. I glanced back. It was there. Fear had overcome my body. My vision blurred and knees wobbled as I fell into the lift. The doors closed...

KATIE McQUILLAN (13)
Beath High School, Cowdenbeath

The Screaming

I was alone, getting out of the shower when I heard something. The layout of my three-floor house is: the ground floor is the kitchen and living room; first floor, my parents' workspace and a bathroom, I think, (I'm not allowed down there because my parents keep personal things in there); second floor is bedrooms and a bathroom. Anyway, I swore someone was screaming from my room. Slowly I crept down the hallway, floor creaking with every step. I could feel the drips of sweat running down my palms. I approached my bedroom. When I realised, wrong floor! Run!

JESSICA DOIG (13)
Beath High School, Cowdenbeath

A Scary Story

You and a group of friends go to a haunted school. You all decide to play hide-and-seek. Two hide and two seek. You seek. You go to a classroom and find there are chains sitting in the middle. Music starts playing and scares you. When the music stops, everything falls silent. Thirty seconds later you hear a scream of a child. A figure starts coming towards you so you run out, trying to escape but the door is locked. You see Sammy and Charlotte stuck in a corner with ghosts. You and Josh become stuck like them. No way to escape.

Emma Louise Keenan (13)
Beath High School, Cowdenbeath

The Spirits Of Halloween

It was Halloween, Sam and his sister Eva approached a house with shattered windows and broken down benches. The house was dark, mysterious and abandoned. They focused their eyes on the door. It forcefully swung open revealing inside of the house. They cautiously walked inside. The door closed and locked behind them. Inside the house was broken ornaments and curtains swaying but there was no wind. Eva clenched onto Sam's arm in fear as they saw a man coming towards them carrying an enchanted box which was shaking wildly. The box opened and took their souls, leaving behind their bodies.

Darci Macdonald (13)
Beath High School, Cowdenbeath

Island Of Macabre

I'm a journalist and years ago I got a crew to report on an island near the English Channel. After everyone slept we awoke to sounds of waves and I went under the water.
I woke, the pain of hunger and bruises covered me. I entered a building of stone to find rusted cells. One cell looked new, I inspected it and found my wife's body.
I felt arms wrap around me and a bag over my head. I was in a room and a horrid creature looked at me, smiling. The walls said, 'No escape, no end, just death.'

Aaron Pullen (12)
Beath High School, Cowdenbeath

Creepy Church

It was Halloween. Myself and Angela decided to visit the creepy church. We reached the doors. It was pitch-black. We had flashlights, we switched them on. We noticed how old it was. There were spiralling stairs; at the top we saw a figure. We saw a mysterious door, we went over to see what was behind it. When we opened it, we saw more stairs. Angela lost her balance. I went down to see if she was all right but she wasn't there! Someone shouted my name, I ran as fast as I could. But I never saw Angela again...

Alisha Barney (13)
Beath High School, Cowdenbeath

The Terrifying Escape Of The Zoo

I entered the zoo at night to look for the statue that had disappeared, when the lights flickered and then went off leaving me alone in the darkness. I couldn't see, so I turned in a circle but when I got back to my starting position there were two green eyes staring at me. I turned and tried to find the gate. The green eyes were firmly locked on me like missiles on a target. I found the gate unlocked and ran through. I turned back to see the green eyes fading into the darkness.

Lewis Campbell (13)
Beath High School, Cowdenbeath

Scary Story

There was an old mansion in a town called Tumbleweed. Two ghost hunters called Josh and Mark decided to investigate. When they entered the mansion the doors slammed behind them, so they decided to look around. Suddenly the lights turned off and a mysterious figure stood in the distance. The lights flickered and the figure was gone. As they ran towards the exit, a secret trap door opened and they fell into a dark room. They saw a book saying: 'You are trapped here forever'. After this John and Mark were never seen again. The were rumoured to be dead.

Ryan Allan (13)
Beath High School, Cowdenbeath

Ghost Train

It was my birthday, me and my friend Iris went to a huge theme park to celebrate. Iris was begging me to go on a ghost train. I was hesitant because it looked terrifying. Iris made me sit at the front, my heart was beating fast. We jolted forwards, faint lights coming from ancient paintings. Everything went pitch-black, the lights flashed back on but Iris wasn't there. I jumped from the ride trying to find Iris, I found her locked up. Just as I was about to sacrifice myself I shot up in my bed, it was all a dream.

STEPHANIE COLL (13)
Beath High School, Cowdenbeath

Mary

I heard a crash in my bathroom. My soap dish had smashed on the floor. Strange events like these had been happening for a while now. I had just got home and I opened the door, soil was everywhere, a plant pot had smashed everywhere. In the soil a name had been drawn out: *'Mary!'* I could feel my heart pounding inside my chest. The bathroom mirror also had a crack in it. I decided to wait on Mary. Suddenly a figure appeared and turned to face me. It let out an ear-piercing scream and disappeared forever.

CIARA DICK (13)
Beath High School, Cowdenbeath

The Haunted House

It was Halloween in 2005. I was going with my friend Sally, when we stumbled across a haunted house. I walked in but Sally left, scared. I continued to look around, then I heard *smash!* from upstairs. I ran upstairs. I looked around then I spotted a broken mirror. I crept nervously around the corner. Then there was a loud yelp coming from the opposite room. I ran to help. There was a white kitten stuck under a bowl. I named the kitten Snowflake. I brought it home, it turned out it was just Snowflake not 'ghosts' at all.

CIARA ROBERTS (12)
Beath High School, Cowdenbeath

The Door

Me and Lily were watching a horror movie marathon when suddenly everything went black, I couldn't see a thing. I next remembered lying on my back covered in dust. I didn't know where I was and I didn't know where Lily was. I stood up and went to the door. I grabbed the handle but it was freezing and burnt my hand. I swiftly took four steps back, clasping my hand tightly to my chest. I finally opened the door, it fell to the back wall. A light blinded me and the next thing I knew, I woke up in bed.

EMILY WILSON (12)
Beath High School, Cowdenbeath

THE HOUSE

I remember the day the paranormal activity was at its worst. My bedroom door opened, my dad appeared from the shadows. His body turned together, his hand rose up, his index finger straightened. He swiped his finger, it sent me flying into my drawers. The sweat dripped off me, I got to my feet and ran for the stairs. He was blocking the doors so I headed for the hatch and climbed through. He grabbed my ankle, I kicked and got away. The walls inside the hatch were closing fast so I picked up the pace. I got out.

GREIG MCHUGH (13)
Beath High School, Cowdenbeath

THE DISAPPEARANCE

The night Liz disappeared was the worst of my life. The night we went into the haunted house. It was Liz's idea, the worst she ever had. It wasn't how you'd imagine haunted places. It was brightly lit with polished suits of armour everywhere. It was beautiful. We started to explore. Everything was going fine until I knocked over a vase. Then the spirits came. Just imagine your worst nightmare with red pinwheeling eyes. That's them. Liz froze. I jumped out the second floor window. The last thing I remembered was Liz's screams. She didn't make it out the house.

ABIGAIL HUMPHRIES (13)
Beath High School, Cowdenbeath

The Lake

Jennie got on the same train to work every day. She passed the same lake over and over again, it was beautiful. She always studied the water and how it moved, except today. There was a black plastic bag floating in the water. People were always ruining the environment and littering so she passed it off as nothing. Another day passed and she noticed two boys in a fishing boat and lots of police trying to get the bag out of the water, she was confused but she saw the headlines: Teen boys find corpse in the lake.

Robyn Thomson (13)
Beath High School, Cowdenbeath

Alone

The darkest hour of the night and I was alone. I clutched onto my dead phone as if it was a symbol of safety. As I walked towards the dark, long, shadowy alleyway, my eyes stretched down the narrow road, stopping on a tall figure just standing there. I turned away almost immediately and dashed down the alleyway. Time seemed to drag no matter how fast I walked and this alleyway was going on forever. Suddenly, I felt hot steamy breath on the back of my neck. As I slowly turned my body, it was him...

Shannon Jackson (16)
Broughton High School, Edinburgh

Bleed To Black

Silence. Just silence. And the ceiling. A grey, grimy, peeling ceiling. Also a draught; a breath crawling across my flesh and leaving a wake of risen skin. I'm bound to something flat and hard and cold. A table? My wrists burn from confinement. The only sound is my laboured breaths. But then it's not. There are footsteps. And the shriek of metal across a wall. Closer and closer and closer. The glint and the blade and the screams. My screams. Skin splitting, scarlet dripping, excruciating, cold eyes. Pain, pain, pain. Bleeding to black... Death?

IONA MACKAY (15)
Broughton High School, Edinburgh

Never Seen Again

It was a dark and spooky night on Halloween. I heard a loud scream and all the lights went out. Me and my dog went home and no lights were on in the town. I went to bed and I had a nightmare. I had lots of scary monsters in my nightmare. Suddenly I woke up and I said it was just a dream, so I went outside my door. It was not a dream. 'Argh!' All the scary monsters that were in my nightmare were outside. They shouted, 'We are hungry.' I was never seen again...

ABBIE JAYNE CALLANDER (13)
Deans Community High School, Livingston

Friday The 13th

Everything was calm at the graveyard where the young girl was visiting her grandmother's grave, but not at the Halloway House nearby. There were loud noises. It was Mad Max hanging a thumb on the orange rundown walls. He didn't know what the young girl was watching him. After seeing Mad Max the young girl ran home to tell her family. Just as she was going Max stood in her way. 'Hi, come with me,' he bellowed loudly. Later that dull, dark, foggy night Mad Max was hanging all of the girl's body parts and she was never seen again.

Erin Todd (13)
Deans Community High School, Livingston

Don't Tell Mum!

I knew mum would be worried but my friends told me to. I had butterflies in my stomach. A shadowy figure swept by me. This abandoned hospital sounded like it was about to crumble. The walls were peeling. A scream like a siren went off, I started to get even more anxious. Mum was trying to call me but she couldn't know I was here. A cold hand covered my mouth pulling me into the darkness. A bag was placed over my head. The cold chain rubbed on my skin. The bag was pulled off slowly. Mum stood before me!

Lara Torrance (13)
Deans Community High School, Livingston

A Frogs Child Is Still A Frog

Mother had told me many times before about what a bad man Dad was. She told me how he used to hang around like a shadow in the streets, and would pick on people from the darkness to do god knows what. He was a vile murderer and I swore to never be like him. If only I'd known before why he was that way. Maybe I wouldn't have judged him. Holding so much power over someone, listening as their screams ran through the night, the tempting taste of their succulent flesh made me see I was just as horrible.

Lucy Young (14)
Deans Community High School, Livingston

Waiting

I graduated four years ago. But I am still here, waiting for my next victim. The paint on the walls is faded, instruments clutter the room. The soundproof ceiling is cracked, bits lay on the floor and the stairs are stained with blood. One rule. No one escapes.
She walked through the corridors, her hands full, back to the room. I waited. I waited until the room went silent. I opened the door. Rope in hand, she laid there peacefully. The last thing I remember was her last breath. I graduated four years ago. But I am still here. Waiting.

Emma Crosbie (14)
Deans Community High School, Livingston

Where Am I?

As I walked through the creepy woods I heard branches snapping and the wind whistling through the gaps of the trees. I started to panic. All of a sudden I started running until a loud bang echoed behind me. I stopped and turned around. I saw a dark shadow. I then heard a deep voice shout, 'Get off, these woods are too dangerous for you to be alone here at this time of day.' I took the creepy man's advice and started to run again. I got out of the woods and didn't know where I was....

COURTNEY MELROSE (12)
Deans Community High School, Livingston

Sam And The Gravestones

It was cold and foggy. Sam was walking home from his friend Max's house. It was nine o'clock. Sam was a twelve-year-old boy and did not live far from his friend. As he walked home he walked past an old abandoned church. He decided to go in and have a look to see what was inside. When he got in he saw lots of gravestones. He had a look around and all of a sudden something popped out of a gravestone *What is it?* Sam thought. Then suddenly, more started to pop out. Would he come out alive?

RACHEL SMITH (12)
Deans Community High School, Livingston

Black Shadow

'Leave, leave, I tell you,' a creepy voice was heard as a bony hand went out to grab him.
'Help me!' he cried, as he was thrown into a pit. His leg ached. 'Hello? Anybody there?' he called desperately. He'd never been alone before. There was nothing to do, or see as the pit was black, but wait.
As the night went on, he was alone but suddenly spooky purple fog started to roll in. He saw a black shadow coming closer. 'Hey, get away from me!' he said. The bony hand came closer - he was the only person taken…

JESSICA MCMULLAN (13)
Drumglass High School, Dungannon

Black Hollow

The dangerous, mysterious town of Black Hollow holds a secret. James McGee has the perfect life working as a policeman in the city and living with his thoughtful girlfriend, Charlotte Woods. However, when he finds a black gun in his cellar, he begins to realise that things are not quite as they seem in the McGee family. An accident leaves James with some startling questions about his past, so he travels to scary Black Hollow to find some answers. At first the people of Black Hollow were nice and calm until darkness fell. That's when the real chaos began.

JOSHUA-JAMES THOMPSON (13)
Drumglass High School, Dungannon

The Terror Way Clown

One foggy night in October we were driving along the deserted roadside. We saw something that had just appeared with the blink of an eye. Something holding a shiny red balloon as if it was made of blood. Charlie got out of the car to see what it was. The thing pulled him into a forest that was beside the roadside. You could hear the screams come from behind...

Sophia McAdorey (12)
Dunclug College, Ballymena

The Griff

Not long, not long before I come to my death. I'm in a forest looking for my family. I was on a scavenger hunt with my family then I came face to face with the evil Griff. His fur was scraggy and rough, that's why we call him the Griff. I thought it was just a legend. It's not long until he gobbles me up and eats me for breakfast.

Abbie McClintock (13)
Dunclug College, Ballymena

David's Fright Night

'David! David!' called a voice from the trees. 'Here! Here!' said the voice.
'What do you want?'
'I warn you do not walk past that old graveyard.'
'Why?'
'You do not want to know.'
'But why?' The voice was gone so David hesitantly tiptoed to the old graveyard, where he looked in. It was dark, old and mystical. He decided not to listen to the person's warning and he went in. The poor chap was never seen again.

Trevor Carson (12)
Dunclug College, Ballymena

Webs

Caleb liked to explore, he had heard of a deserted island. He got to the dock and headed to the island. He had noticed fog. He got to the island and climbed in the cave, he saw many paths but only one stood out for him. He walked in the tunnel and he saw an enormous spider, it caught him and wrapped him in a web and tore all his body parts out!

Connor Swann (13)
Dunclug College, Ballymena

The Three Ghostlings' First Christmas

On Halloween Night, all the ghouls and ghosts are out stealing sweets and treats from all the boys and girls, it's only natural for them to steal on their holiday... But after Halloween has passed, when all the undead have to return to their graves, all is sad until next year... Of course not for three little ghostlings who just won't wait until next year. So on Christmas Eve, when all the presents are all delivered, the three ghostlings steal all the gifts they can find and absorb the sweets and treats from the stockings... until they are caught.

Alex Dionne Kelly (13)
Dunclug College, Ballymena

Room Of Fear!

Drip, drip, drip... That awful sound repeated, scratching at my raw nerves! Creaking, the door opening again, dragging footsteps moved past me to the table. My eyes opened for an instant, but only fear rushed in. The flickering dim light did not allow me to see the full horror of what was happening to my friend, but I knew. I lay hidden, the sound of his blood dripping onto the cold dirty concrete floor, the thick stench of it filling my lungs with each shallow breath I took. I knew what was to come... Would I be next?

India McNiece (13)
Dunclug College, Ballymena

Where Is John?

'John is that you?' *Bang! Crash! Boom!* The noise stops at once. I get out of bed, the floorboards creak. Again I say, 'Is it you John?' He doesn't reply. I enter his room as quiet as I can. 'John, where are you? Stop it, you're scaring me.'
Bang! A sharp pain on the back of my head. Everything goes black...

AARON ADAIR (13)
Dunclug College, Ballymena

Hallway Of Terror

It was silent. A hallway filled with darkness and the echo of everything that moved. His loud, slow footsteps walked up with fear to the large door that was waiting for him. The lights twitching, and his footsteps got louder as he built up his nerves to walk in. A cold wave of terror ripped up his spine. He opened the creaking, old door to see wet footsteps walking with no body...

SARAH MCANALLY (13)
Dunclug College, Ballymena

NIGHT BEFORE CHRISTMAS

Timmy was sleeping very peacefully, until he heard a noise. His face glowed with excitement as he thought it was Santa. Timmy was very much mistaken because a mass-murderer was just below him. He crept down the stairs. 'Santa? Is that you?' he said while searching for what he thought was Santa. He opened the door and... *bang!*

ADAM BOYD (13)
Dunclug College, Ballymena

THE LURKING PRESENCE

The weather outside was awful. Me and my friend, Lorraine, were going to have to stay in the church for longer. The headstones were crumbling under the rain. 'I'm going outside to see if the reception is better,' Lorraine said. I nodded, but I didn't want her to go.
The atmosphere around me was uncomfortable. I began to hear movement around me, but Lorraine was still outside. Staring at the door I waited for her to return. Footsteps began to approach me and a hand curled around my shoulder. 'Lorraine?' I asked, nervously.

COREY STEELE (13)
Dunclug College, Ballymena

My Story

Hi, I am Sam and I'm going to tell you a scary story. I was passing the gloomy graveyard when I saw a sinister black figure looming ominously in the distance. I felt drawn to go towards it, but when I got closer it disappeared in a mist of swirling fog. A shiver spiralled up my spine like an electric bolt. I galloped wildly home, sweat dripping off my brow like melting ice. When I woke in the morning Mum told me old Joe had died last night. Then I realised! Old Joe's ghost had been wandering aimlessly last night.

JACK LUKE (12)
Dunclug College, Ballymena

The Haunted House

Me and Issac were slowly creeping towards the house. 'I'm nervous,' said Issac.
'Don't worry,' I muttered. Ivy smothered the house. I went up onto the patio and looked through the window. I saw a creepy woman with dark hair beside a cauldron. I turned around and my friend Issac was gone. My heart was beating like a drum. It felt like it was going to burst out of my chest. I heard something. 'Issac is that you buddy?' I whispered. I ran to the door and opened it and I ran in the house. 'Issac are you here buddy?'

JOHN DUNDEE (13)
Dunclug College, Ballymena

The House On The Hill

The man crunched up the winding path leading to a derelict old house. Mist fogged around the black creaking gates. It was a dark night and it was the only place around. He had no choice but to stay the night. As he opened the heavy oak doors he called out, 'Hello?' Nobody answered, the house stayed silent and unforgiving. Setting himself in the corner he felt a drop of liquid hit his back. It was blood. He jumped up and looked around, suddenly drawing level with two bloodshot eyes, the inside of them a vivid orange colour...

Eva McAloon (12)
Hermitage Academy, Helensburgh

The Fear Of The Unknown

Whoosh, whoosh, the trees blew as the rain bounced down onto the windows. He could see the fear in himself as he daydreamed in the mirror. Stepping outside feeling dead inside. However, as he approached the door everything went numb. He felt nothing! When he knocked, the door just opened, It creaked. He walked in and came face to face with this thing, pure green eyes, no whites, stinky breath and purple skin. But what was it? Shivering, he walked back. The door slammed shut and it locked. It growled as it walked towards him and opened its arms...

Emma Louise Green (12)
Hermitage Academy, Helensburgh

The Man In The Mirror

The room was dark, dusty and cluttered. There were white sheets over everything: paintings, jars, china, books and boxes full of the kids' old toys and clothes. An ordinary room during the day but at night something happened in that room, something strange. Margo crept up the stairs to the attic that lay behind locked doors. The candlelight was no match for the darkness that lurked. The floorboards creaked, Margo shot around. There it was, maybe not very obvious but the silhouette was clear, it was him, the man in the painting, the man in the mirror.

Madeline Bridget Fuller (12)
Hermitage Academy, Helensburgh

The Getaway

Before her stood a tall lanky shadow. It started walking towards her so that she could make out its face. She saw a flowing, sickly, oily, black cape trail onto the pavement. His blood-red eyes were in perfect unison as they darted around, evidently looking for something or someone. His pale white face looked haunting. He made a devilish grin. His pure white teeth glimmered in the moonlight. He also had fangs and blood was dribbling down onto his chin. Then suddenly, he pounced onto Morgan in a swift cat-like motion just before the serpent-like tongue licked his lips.

Jenny Guy (12)
Hermitage Academy, Helensburgh

No Escape

She knew she wasn't alone, something was lurking in the darkness. She closed her eyes and hoped this was just her imagination. She opened her eyes and all of a sudden she saw a figure standing before her, it had deep hollowed eyes that were penetrating her soul, the smell in the room was now reeking of death. The dark mysterious figure began to manoeuvre its body towards her. She felt a raw chill down her spine as the figure continued to move towards her. She was cornered, there was no escape...

CAITLYN MIA WRIGHT (11)
Hermitage Academy, Helensburgh

Knock, Knock

I stumbled through the trees, thorns ripping at my clothes, but I knew I couldn't stop. The thing was still after me. Up ahead I could make out the house. When I got to the door I opened it and slammed it shut behind me. As soon as I got in I locked the door and all the windows. When suddenly, *knock, knock.* I cowered on the armchair. Then it came again.

Knock. Knock. I noticed a mouse hole which hadn't been there before. I went closer and peered in. Suddenly a grey, spindly hand shot out and grabbed me.

ROWAN MCKAY-HUBBARD (12)
Hermitage Academy, Helensburgh

Mist

He could see it looming out of the decaying woods. The rundown mansion had an eerie feel to it. He looked up at the sky. There was no chance of making it home tonight, so rather than staying out in the cold he went inside. As he stepped in the doors slammed behind him. He was walking down the corridor when he heard the roaring of a fire coming from behind the huge oak doors and he knew that night he was not alone.

MILES WILLIAMS (11)
Hermitage Academy, Helensburgh

Trapped!

Crash! It came from downstairs. I went to check, but there was nothing there apart from broken pieces of glass on the floor. But then I turned around; there was blood on the wall saying, 'You're next!' I went to walk forward but then the lights shattered and fell on the floor. I tried to run but the doors were locked. I tried to call someone but there was no signal. I couldn't do anything. My last idea was to break a window but they wouldn't break. I then realised I was stuck in this house with a ghost.

KORY ALLAN (12)
Hermitage Academy, Helensburgh

The Death Diary

She stood there, paralysed in the corridor, scared at what was lurking in the darkness. She shivered in the dark, breezy air that circled around her. At the end of the corridor she saw faint outlines of what looked liked a gruesome ghost patrolling the house. The shadow edged closer, she became frozen with fear. She knew what was going to happen. She knew it was the end. The ghost caught sight of her and now he was coming directly for her. The ghost had a bloody pocket knife, ready to slash her throat. This was it, it was over....

JODIE MACKAY (12)
Hermitage Academy, Helensburgh

The Bouncy Castle

One fine night, there was a party at the Bruces' house. The Bruces had a son called Jack. Jack was crazy, nice, annoying and always wanted a girlfriend. His dad had ordered a bouncy castle for the children. Of course, every one of Jack's friends and cousins were busy so he had it all to himself. Turns out, only his granny and two grandparents turned up and they never stopped chatting. He saw a bouncy castle come to the garden. The creepy music came on and before he could run, he got swallowed and he was never seen again. Mwahaha!

DREW BEGLEY (12)
Kilwinning Academy, Kilwinning

A Frightful Christmas Eve

One dark, foggy Christmas Eve, Susie heard a noise from the woods near her house. Susie popped on her boots and coat and headed for the woods. Once she arrived at the woods, she heard screams of torture and something touched her shoulder. She was startled. A shiver ran down her spine and coldness hit her. She saw dark frightful eyes staring at her. *No,* she thought, *just my imagination*. Then she saw someone. Someone big, fat and scary. Then Susie realised it was Santa! She went and helped him back on his way!

Eilidh Smith
Kilwinning Academy, Kilwinning

The Old Graveyard!

Jake opened the rustic graveyard gate and stepped inside. He wandered around, winding through the cobblestone path and reached the top of the tallest hills in the graveyard where an old graveyard lay, crumbling to pieces. He reached out and brushed his hand against the engraving. Suddenly he felt the ground open and swallow him. Rushing to the ground he braced himself for the impact. There, under the ground, Jake could hardly see. Goblins ran to him and tied him up. Then after a day he escaped and returned home. When he arrived home he forgot everything.

Halle Lara Duncan (12)
Kilwinning Academy, Kilwinning

The Antique Shop!

My granny took me to an antique shop, it was mysterious and dull. I was looking around and I saw a freaky doll. It had big black eyes, purple lips and puffy red cheeks. Suddenly my granny disappeared. The doors shut, the room went silent... The doll's head spun, it marched towards me. Its friends came out of drawers with needles and thread shouting, 'I'm coming for you.' I ran. I hid under the chair... The doll pinned me to the floor, shaved my hair off, sewed my lips together and before I knew it I was a doll!

ELLYS RAE (12)
Kilwinning Academy, Kilwinning

The Haunted Playpark

The wind howled as a group of five lost boys wandered into an old play park. 'Argh!' One got trapped in a tyre swing and everyone else ran away. They ran all around the park and when they got back to the tyre swing, their friend was a skeleton and someone else was missing. The other three were petrified. There was utter silence until... *boom!* Another blew up, three down, two to go...

JAMIE BEGLEY (12)
Kilwinning Academy, Kilwinning

Dark Shadows

One dark, stormy and foggy night a boy called Tim had no friends. He did try to make friends, but everyone just kept walking away, so he just ended up running away. He raced to the woods, next to his house. As he got to the woods he noticed some strange shadows which he thought were dogs at first, until they started moving. That's when he saw that the shadows weren't dogs, as they were much taller when they stood on their back legs. All of a sudden a gush of wind blew past and the shadows had gone.

SPENCER MCNEIL (12)
Kilwinning Academy, Kilwinning

The Boy And The Mansion

Bang! As I walked in the old scary mansion the door slammed closed behind me. It was cold, dark and full of cobwebs. I suddenly heard voices and it made me shake with fear. I thought someone was going to kill me. Each different room was scary in its own way. One room was filled with snakes. The only light I had was the moonlight shining through the window. The voices got louder and louder and my heart got faster and faster. I started running down the stairs and out the door and suddenly it all stopped.

JACK BRUCE (12)
Kilwinning Academy, Kilwinning

The 4th Floor

There's a rumour at our school that there's a fourth floor but it's impossible, there are only three floors!
It was a normal day, but today the lift had broken again! It always seemed to break down. The janitor wasn't a very talkative person, never seemed to smile. Anyway, he decided to not say or he must have forgotten. Ayda and I went in the lift to art. Suddenly the lift made a bang! And there it was, the fourth floor all empty and abandoned. I heard voices. We swung round, the door slammed shut! And there it was! 'Run!'

JENNY CRAIG (12)
Kilwinning Academy, Kilwinning

The Haunted Street

I always knew this place was haunted. As I crept through the damp street, my teeth chattering, my spine crawling, my legs shaking with fear, I knew this wasn't over. I could sense it, ever since I went there my life had changed... A man, tall, dark mysterious. Suddenly, the wind picked up, the street lights flickered. It was happening right here, right now. Screams, shrieks, howls. All these sounds filled my head. It was controlling me, shutters clanging, the faint whistle of wolves and flutters of bats. Emerging from the fog a hand grabbed me. Was it the end?

LAURYN GRAY (12)
Kilwinning Academy, Kilwinning

Movie Scene?

Paul started walking towards the city centre one dark, wet, windy night. He noticed some things were strange. Doors were banging and he heard groaning noises. He saw shadowy figures and ran towards them. He started to recognise what they were. 'Zombies,' he whispered to himself. He ran into a building, pulled the door closed and gazed out of the dirty window, terror-stricken. He opened his eyes wide and stared straight ahead. Then he heard banging on the door and he saw them come closer to the window. As the zombies reached the door the director shouted, 'Cut!'

JACK MACMILLAN STEVENSON (11)
Kilwinning Academy, Kilwinning

Untitled

Paul sat on the bench in the hot sunshine. He had tided the grass on his wife's grave. Now he could relax. Suddenly he felt a cold breeze but couldn't figure out where it was coming from. He noticed that the flowers on one of the graves looked disturbed and for some odd reason there was a shadow on the grave. He felt a hand touch his shoulder. Paul thought whoever it was... was visiting a dead relative but then he realised the hand was cold, dead cold...

JACK DAVISON (12)
Kilwinning Academy, Kilwinning

The Monster

One night there was a young boy creeping through a graveyard. He could feel a cold breeze roaming through the gravestones. The young boy could feel it getting colder and colder. Suddenly, he felt a warm breath on top of his head. He looked up, there was a big green monster. It began to get closer to the boy. The boy took another look at it and then he decided to run. Full pelt he ran through the gravestones, he could hear the monster's thudding footsteps behind him. The monster grabbed the young boy. 'Help!' he roared...

CHARLIE SPENCE (12)
Kilwinning Academy, Kilwinning

One Stormy Abandoned House

One stormy day, there was an abandoned house. A group of teenagers climbed up and there was a smashed window, vandalised walls and doors. A boy called John started to run. He fell and burst his knee open. He felt a dash of wind go past him so he shouted all of his friends but he heard no reply so he shouted again. He heard no reply again. He felt something tap his shoulder so he tried to get away but it felt like he was sticking to the floor. Then all the lights turned on, it was his friend.

BRANDON SUTTERFIELD (12)
Kilwinning Academy, Kilwinning

The Graveyard Ghost!

One foggy, windy night I was walking through the woods when I saw a faded shadow in the distance. At first I thought it was my brother but as I got closer it disappeared. So I kept on walking even though I was scared. Then suddenly I heard someone screaming. I ran into an abandoned shed. Suddenly I was freezing cold and it felt as if someone was blowing on my neck. I didn't know what to do. I couldn't breathe. Then someone slammed the door and the window swung open. I was terrified. I saw a ghost!

TEGAN HIGGINS (11)
Kilwinning Academy, Kilwinning

Possessed Doll

It was a dark and foggy night, Jemima and Jimmy were walking through the woods when they found a doll. They picked it up, realised it was broken and threw it back on the ground. They went home that night to find the doll on Jemima's bed. Jemima got really freaked out about this and ran to tell Jimmy. The two decided that the doll was possessed and that it was best to throw the doll away, but hours later they saw the doll on the porch in their back garden. That was the last time they were seen!

CHLOE MARION-ELIZABETH WALKER (12)
Kilwinning Academy, Kilwinning

The Hellsing House

The tree fell, blocking the road from the Hellsing house. The stone path I walked led up to a large wooden door with brass handles. I turned the handle and pushed it open. It led to a room with stairs going up the middle. I walked up the stairs. 'Hello?' I said casually, knowing this place was abandoned anyway. Once I got to the top of the stairs I turned to see the room had changed. The stairs were gone and in their place was a stone wall. I still can't find my way out of Hellsing.

Denise Gatherer (12)
Kilwinning Academy, Kilwinning

Fairground Frights

One cold evening Callum and Emily were on a date. They decided to go to an abandoned fairground. It was mossy and rusty though they decided to go on the wheel. It started to creak and spin uncontrollably. They heard laughter behind them. Emily turned around to see nothing! The wheel slowly halted. They got off. As they stepped off the mud squelched under their feet and the mist grew thicker. Callum felt Emily's hand on his shoulder but it was a cold, wet hand, why? They heard whispers coming from behind them. It was getting closer. What was it?

Emma Gillan (12)
Kilwinning Academy, Kilwinning

The Unexpected

At first the beach looked lovely. Sun umbrellas of all colours dotted in the sand. Families started to feel cold as a big wind came and blew sand in their faces. More wind came and the lifeguard waved a red flag to tell everyone in the sea to come out urgently. Everyone rushed out. Then the wave got bigger and the sky got darker, sand blowing everywhere. People tried to hold their stuff. Sun-loungers getting pulled into the sea by the wind. The water churned up seaweed, foam, sand and bits of plastic. Their holidays seemed to be over.

RACHAEL MCAULAY (12)
Kilwinning Academy, Kilwinning

The Mysterious Music

One night two sisters called Poppy and Holly were walking through the woods to find some branches for the fire. Suddenly it went silent. They held hands because they were scared but then they heard loud music coming from somewhere unclear. They decided to be brave and search for wherever the music was coming from. The two sisters split up to find the music. Poppy walked away in the other direction then she heard a scream. Poppy shouted, 'Holly! Holly, where are you?' There was no answer. And Holly was nowhere to be found...

LAUREN BOYD (11)
Kilwinning Academy, Kilwinning

The Awakened

One night in a caravan park a boy named John needed the toilet but his toilet didn't flush so he went out to the toilet block. He walked there fine but when he tried to get back he got lost and noticed something glowing. He knew it was probably nothing but one pair was different. They were bigger and greener. He walked around and the eyes followed him. He found the way back to the caravan so he started to run. When he reached the van he turned. The eyes were bigger and much closer...

Ryan Morris (12)
Kilwinning Academy, Kilwinning

The Supermarket

Why are busy places so creepy when they're empty? Joe walked through the derelict supermarket. The light cut through the dusty air. Lumps of plaster crumbled and fell off the wall. When it landed it echoed through the empty building. Joe saw a door slowly open and a dim light crept through. Joe walked through the door and down the empty corridor. Music began to play quietly as if someone was winding up a jack-in-the-box. He continued towards a second open door; something glistened behind it. Before Joe could see round, *bang!* Something got him...

Ethan Logan (12)
Kilwinning Academy, Kilwinning

Beam Of Doom

The hard rain beats on the roof. I'm on the beam and my sight is beginning to get blurry and then I fall on the back of my head and lie there for a couple of seconds before being plunged into a world of darkness. I begin to wake up in a pile of blood. The gym is empty. After a few seconds I begin to see figures dancing I get up trying to avoid them but they are getting closer, they are calling Bella. My name. I'm getting scared and then I fall and never get up again.

ELLIE BUCHANAN
Kilwinning Academy, Kilwinning

The Graveyard

It was midday when Cailin decided to visit her gran's grave. She bought a bunch of flowers and went to the grave. She slowly laid the flowers down and turned away. But as she turned, she saw a man waving at her. Cailin slowly put her arm up and waved back.
The next day Cailin went back to the grave and there was a different bunch of flowers on the grave, and the man was waving again but this time he kept shouting, 'Hello.' Cailin was wondering who it was and why the flowers kept changing, but she never found out.

TEGAN LONG (12)
Kilwinning Academy, Kilwinning

The Museum

Kelly stays at the museum after closing time. She goes to see the old royal stuff. She walks past the animals, Egypt, then finally the dinosaurs before she comes to the royal things. When she walks past the dinosaur room there is nothing in there. She walks in curiously. Just then she freezes, she feels a cold dead breath chill her back. She turns around to see double skeletons of T-rexes. One has a bone. She grabs it, the dinosaur doesn't look too happy. She drops it then the dinosaurs pick her up and stretch and stretch her...

Emily Nelson (11)
Kilwinning Academy, Kilwinning

The Horror Hotel

I was running in the dark. A man jumped out from a doorway. He had a black coat on and half of his face was ripped off. I ran off into the woods. After running for a time I found an old hotel in the woods. It was big with smashed windows. The door was all kicked open and it had a tree growing through it. I walked in and half the staircase had snapped off. In the middle of the floor there was an old man sitting in a rocking chair holding a rabbit. He was dead.

Taylor Ellis (12)
Kilwinning Academy, Kilwinning

Mossburn

A black crow squawked on top of the gateway to Mossburn Mansion. Its wings were fluttering as it flew up to a window.
It made its way through the dreary hallways and past a pool of blood on a wall, which thin streams of rich crimson crept away from.
The ground was littered with flakes of white paint that used to be a part of the whiteness that lived on the walls. The crow was going to meet the one who sits on the Throne of Bones. He who resides in the basement of Mossburn Mansion: The Truculent Tentacled Terror.

Myles Quinn (14)
Malone College, Belfast

Just Skin And Bones

They used to say she was just skin and bones, but she was once captivating with red hair and green clover eyes. We married in a church in Vienna, one whose altar preached more about the church's riches than the priest's fine garments. Yet the bells sang deeply, its music vibrating the strings of my heart. As our prime passed onto our children, we started hearing those comments more often. Just skin and bones. But to me, she's still beautiful. Truthfully, I don't recognise her skeletal frame beside me, nor the smell seeping from the rotting marrow of her bones.

Luke Mulholland (15)
St Patrick's Academy, Lisburn

Untitled

I got a chill down my spine as the thunder and lightning clashed, it was a big loud bang. I needed to get under a roof as it started to rain and hailstone, it was horrific weather. I saw some light in the distance, it looked like an old abandoned house. As I got closer to the house, I heard a creak on the wooden floor from inside the house. I thought someone was inside. I opened the rusty door and it was unlocked. I shouted, 'Hello.' The door slammed behind me. No one replied, then a man stepped out...

MATTHEW MCGRATH (13)
St Ronan's College, Lurgan

Living Nightmare

Silence. Nothing to be heard but the occasional hoot of ravens. Then suddenly thunder crashed! I came across a small cottage completely isolated. I sat down in a small chair beside the fire. Peaceful. Then *crash!* The door slammed shut and the window flew open. My heart thumping out of my chest, I heard footsteps. I turned, but no one was there. Or so I thought. Blood trickled down my face. I had been struck. Everything went black. I woke up screaming. It was all a dream. Then I saw a scar on my face. Was it a dream?

AIMEE MCVEIGH (14)
St Ronan's College, Lurgan

The Creepy Forest

Rain was pouring and the shadows of the trees looked like walking monsters. I couldn't find my way out, every direction was full of endless trees. I heard a big bang and went to see what it was. I ran for half a mile but I couldn't see anything. But then I saw a wooden shack with a fire and no one around. I went into the shack to get some warmth and to see if there was something to eat. I was warm but there was nothing to eat. Then suddenly, I heard a scary growling noise behind me...

AARON CASEY (13)
St Ronan's College, Lurgan

The Smile

I was running. My heart was beating faster. My breaths were getting heavier. I heard a creepy giggle. Then there was an eerie silence. I slowly turned around. Gulp. There they were. Heads down. Hair in pony tails. Wearing ragged white dresses. I took a step back. I was horrified. What was happening? Would I somehow get out of this nightmare? Only if I could find my way out of this maze. I took a left. It was a mistake. A dead end. I turned around. They were there. Synchronised steps towards me. Giggling. Their heads went up. Their smiles...

DAIRE CAMPBELL (13)
St Ronan's College, Lurgan

Enter At Your Own Risk

The isolated, deserted castle crept into view. The trees seemed to whisper. The old, torn curtains escaped through the shattered windows. The castle seemed to entice people to come inside. That's just the way Mike went in and... never... came... out. The door squeaked open and Mike entered, oblivious to all. When he stepped inside, a blood-curdling shiver crept up his spine. He wanted to get out. *Bang!* The door shut! He was stuck inside, and petrified. What was he going to do? Suddenly, he heard suspicious footsteps and next thing he knew a hand grasped his leg...

Sian Heaney (14)
St Ronan's College, Lurgan

The Sandman

Where am I? On no! Why did I let myself sleep? I knew my stepmother was going to do this to me. I should have thought. Oh no! Everything is turning pitch-black, the spell, it's starting to take its toll. He's coming, I can feel it. I can't wake up! I can feel footsteps coming. His hypnotising song, pulling me in. He's here, I can hear his rasping breath. This is it. I'm dead. Please God forgive me for the sins I've made. He lifts me on to my back, put our mouths together and destroys my spirit...

Eva Callaghan
St Ronan's College, Lurgan

All Alone

Bang! My car hit the tree but the airbag saved me. Then I left the car out in the woods. Alone. But I saw a building in the shadow and there it was, a moss covered, old church. I entered and the floorboards creaked under my feet with each step. I could hear music but as soon as I noticed it, it stopped. It was dead silent. As I watched in horror, my eyes adjusted and I saw all the bodies. Then I heard wind slash right behind me. I turned around and nothing. Then it pulled my feet.

ARNIJS MARTINSONS (14)
St Ronan's College, Lurgan

One Cold Night

The weather was very grim on this cold Sunday night. It had been snowing non-stop all day and the streets were now filled with thick ice and snow making it difficult to get anywhere on foot or in a car. It was almost completely silent except for the hooting of the owls and the wind howling. You could also hear dogs barking occasionally in the distance. I continued to trudge through the cold snow when suddenly, I tripped and fell on the ice causing my head to bleed. I got up and suddenly a gloved hand grabbed me.

EIMHIN DERBY (14)
St Ronan's College, Lurgan

Untitled

It's raining heavily now, I have been following the footsteps for some time. The rain has wiped them clean from the dirt track in the forest. It's getting dark and the battery on my torch is dead. I'm alone in the dark. *Crack!* A loud sound comes from behind me. 'Hello?' It echoes through the dark forest. The creak of the tree in front of me makes me jump but as I jump back, I hit a person. It's him. I start to run but I can't see. I trip and fall into a ditch. That's it, I'm dead!

NIALL MCSTRAVICK (14)
St Ronan's College, Lurgan

Spug's Nightmare!!

It was a frosty night and *bang!* the window shut. I went to see who it was but I could only see Spug starting his car. He was going to take his dog Dippy for a walk. I got back into bed and I heard someone downstairs. I didn't want to go down in case I got attacked by Spug's dog. I finally decided to sneak downstairs and when I got down, I walked into the kitchen and saw Dippy lying on the floor, dead, with blood all over the place.

AARON JOSEPH MCGIBBON (14)
St Ronan's College, Lurgan

Forgotten

The sharp, brisk winds whisked through the mossy, bare trees. I was all alone. I wandered up to an abandoned shack, hoping for shelter. There were broken windows, a worn roof and a large oak door. I creaked open the door and tiptoed in. It was all so quiet. I closed the door behind me. It was empty, there was nothing but an old rocking chair. An array of moonlight sprawled over the chair, when suddenly it began to rock... No one was there... I felt a cold wind blow, then the large oak door burst open...

AARON O'HANLON (13)
St Ronan's College, Lurgan

The Dark Brotherhood

We arrived at the Dark Brotherhood Sanctuary, the home of the creepy supernatural killers. I looked at the door, it was red and dark. I looked closer at it. There was a red hand made with blood. I was about to touch it when it started to talk. It said to draw blood so I cut my hand and pressed it onto the red hand mark. I watched as my arm slowly turned red and black. My veins turned black. I felt my memories fade away. 'My eyes!' I had gone blind. My eyes opened. The Devil grabbed me...

JOSEPH TONY MALLON (14)
St Ronan's College, Lurgan

Insane

People say he went insane from alcohol, drugs and horrible beatings from his father. He murders his victims by chopping their bodies, mincing them and then covers their local church in the remains. His trademark is to write their names with their blood over the altar. He chooses his victims carefully, if you're just walking alone *snap!* You're captured. He's got away with 37 murders of young women. He doesn't want to kill his victims, he's just insane. Don't walk alone because it could happen to you. You can't kill him... because *I'm* already dead.

Zoe Traynor (14)
St Ronan's College, Lurgan

Revenge!

John stumbled into the bathroom and flicked on the light. He jumped with a start. Elizabeth, his dead wife, was staring at him in the mirror. He asked, barely able to speak, 'What are you doing here?'
'I've come back for my revenge,' she said with a devilish smirk. He went to see a doctor thinking he was imagining all this, and got medication hoping it would help. At first, the medication seemed to be doing its job, but, after a few weeks he saw her again at the corner of his eye....

Louise McGrath (14)
St Ronan's College, Lurgan

A Little Boy And An Old Man

A storm was creeping in. He wouldn't be back in time, it was too dark. He was in the graveyard in the country. Suddenly, a loud noise started. All he could hear were loud footsteps. He turned around and old man was shouting 'Help! Help!' But the boy couldn't see. It was pitch black. He turned around and he could hear church bells, gates banging and children singing. 'La la la la la.' They stopped singing that and they started again by singing, 'One, two, he's coming for you.' So he ran home but he fell over.

SHANNA MCCORD (13)
St Ronan's College, Lurgan

Graveyard

One night on a graveyard shift, I saw an old woman who was withering away like acid on wood. She rose from her grave and started to slowly walk over to me. As she got closer, I realised it was my P6 English teacher called Miss O'Kane. I started running away and as I got further away she started speeding up. I went to meet my friends Ciara and Purdy. As we walked to the grave, we saw her wandering about so we got close but then I shoved Purdy in and she started to eat him so I killed her.

JOSH DEVLIN (14)
St Ronan's College, Lurgan

Trapped

I was trapped. Stuck in my own head. In my room. Alone reading all these horror stories. What a dumb thing to do, right? I was going out of my mind, I failed to get my head around where this scream had come from. Moments before, my house was in dead silence. Finally plucking up the courage to go and investigate. Creeping down the steps, tumbling over my own feet in fright. I got to the kitchen and to my surprise, I saw my mother and father. Good prank!

Niamh Ellen McDonald (16)
St Ronan's College, Lurgan

The Apocalypse

In the year 2030 the apocalypse has spread. The fight for survival rages on between the living and the undead. Three men burst through a door into a building, block the staircase with anything they can and use the second floor as a safe house. 'We have to make it out of here and cure this illness.'
'Those fireworks may come in handy for an escape.' They spend the night in the building. When they wake they find the building is overrun by zombies. They use the fireworks as a distraction but fail to escape and are devoured by the creatures.

Patrick McShane (15)
St Ronan's College, Lurgan

A Haunted House

It was a dark, foggy night. A young girl and her friends were walking down a long lane not able to see what was in front of them. The lane was spooky with the wind whistling through the trees. The girls walked and came to a massive spooky house. The long blowy trees reflected the light coming from the moon. They walked closer to the large, dark house feeling spooked out. They kicked the door open and slowly but quietly walked in. The door shut behind them loudly with a bang!

MEABH MCSTRAVICK (13)
St Ronan's College, Lurgan

The Cold-Blooded Killer

I came home, turned on the TV and the news came on. They said one of the most dangerous persons had escaped the asylum. They warned people to close all their doors and windows and to double their security. Later that night, I was getting ready for bed. I turned off the light and got into bed. I heard deep, fast breathing. It was the escapist. He got up and was breathing over my face. What will happen? What will he do to me? Will he kill me or will he take me hostage?

SEÁN WALSH (13)
St Ronan's College, Lurgan

The Masked Man

Out of nowhere, a man jumped out with a knife and began chasing Erin down the alleyways of Belfast. It was a cold, stormy night and Erin was almost slipping with every step as she ran as fast as she could. The man had a machete and was closing in on Erin. She was still miles from home. He caught up and pulled his mask off and...
'Cut!' shouted the director.

JACK HANNON
St Ronan's College, Lurgan

The Shadows

As the shadows crept in my nightmare soon became my reality. The man in my dreams, the man who was destined to kill me, was right in front of me. I ran as fast as my skinny little legs could take me, but he was too fast. He had dark hair and was pale white. I came to the end of the long alleyway. I panicked so I screamed. Just then, I realised that this was no dream, this was real. Straight away I knew. I knew what was going to happen to me. I was going to die tonight.

AINE LAVERY MCKEOWN
St Ronan's College, Lurgan

Jamie And The Beast

Jamie couldn't believe how things had gone so wrong for him. He remembered falling behind. He saw a fascinating animal and completely focused on it when something grabbed onto him. Jamie was having none of it. Jamie wrestled with the beast. The wind was howling, it was pitch-black. He had no way out but he did not worry. He ran straight ahead but tripped and fell. He was bleeding. The beast rushed forward...

HUGH HANNON (12)
St Ronan's College, Lurgan

The Shadow

She woke up in a dark room. Dust and blood everywhere. She didn't know where to go. She could tell that she was in some sort of building. She checked every room, but nothing was there. Then, she saw something out of the corner of her eye. She shouted, 'Hi, my name is Dearbhla, so you know where I am?' She saw it again, it kept popping up and then disappearing. She ran, trying to get out. She turned a corner and it was right in front of her. There was no escape.

TARA HARVEY (13)
St Ronan's College, Lurgan

The 'Haunted' House!

Last night my friends and I went to this 'haunted' house, to see if we could stay in it for one night. It was pitch-black. As we entered, we walked up the stairs. Every step we took, the stairs creaked. Suddenly, we heard the door creak open then slam shut. We heard someone scream. That's when we knew we weren't alone! It was 1am and we were tired so I went down the stairs to close the door that the wind blew open. I turned round and suddenly saw a man walking towards me with a knife...

Andrea McKavanagh
St Ronan's College, Lurgan

Sleep Paralysis

After a long night of work, I fell into a darkened sleep. When I woke from a delusional sleep, I couldn't move anything but my eyes. I looked around. There were petrifying, dark and mysterious figures in the corner of my bedroom but they were high in numbers. They were like a Spanish Armada. As they got closer to my bed, my heart was pounding like a fast car on the road. As each hand started to reach for my heart, I was awakened by my roommate Shea as I was screaming.

John McAlinden (13)
St Ronan's College, Lurgan

The Demon Dogs

Jamie and Hugh saw something unexpected. It was this weird looking dog. It had glowing eyes and sharp teeth. Jamie said, 'Hugh, do you see that dog?'
'Yes!' There were more. The dogs started to turn into demon dogs. Jamie and Hugh split. One jumped on Hugh but he easily knocked it out. They hid in the graveyard where none of the demon dogs could get them but then, there was a massive growl. Jamie and Hugh ran for their lives but there were too many demon dogs for Jamie and Hugh. Both got bitten...

JAMIE MENARY (13)
St Ronan's College, Lurgan

Escaping The Care Home

The horn beeped as I got dragged into the care home. Old Mr Wink was standing, staring. 5 o'clock was dinner, but I said I wasn't hungry. Really, I just went to Mr Wink's office to steal the spare front door key. Next thing I knew, it was 9 o'clock and we had to go to bed. I stayed up waiting for Mr Wink to go to bed. I crept downstairs. *Crash!* The bookshelf collapsed. Mr Wink came running, inspected and then went back to bed. I unlocked the door. A cold, wrinkly hand covered my mouth...

KATY MAGENNIS (12)
St Ronan's College, Lurgan

The Dangerous Door

One night, a girl called Rebekah was with her sister and they were home alone. It was Friday the 13th. She heard a knock on the door so she went to answer it. No one was there. The door knocked again. She got so annoyed that she shouted, 'Who's doing this?'
A creepy voice said, 'Look behind you.' She was really scared. She turned around slowly. She was stabbed and dragged away with blood dripping.

Niall McCann (12)
St Ronan's College, Lurgan

Writing On The Walls

Blood dripping from the walls like crimson tears of depressed souls tortured to death. I lay there with cuts and bruises not knowing what was next, what horrors awaited, what fatal torture would befall me. I tried to free myself from the shackles that restrained me to the sorrowful walls of retribution. I started losing power in my body as the blood slowly descended to the floor. As my conscience collapsed and my soul deteriorated into an empty hole, the door opened and in came a dark figure, it was...

Oisin Fitzpatrick (16)
St Ronan's College, Lurgan

Dark Forest

There are dark silhouettes all around me. I try to escape but I've nowhere to go. Suddenly the leaves are crunching and twigs are snapping. Turning around, I see nothing except darkness. I can feel a presence beside me, yet my feet seem glued to the ground. I need to escape, I need to hide. There is a sharp pain in my chest, a substance staining my dirty clothes. A hot breath on my neck warms my freezing body. Why am I unable to make a sound? A barely audible voice whispers in my ear, 'I'm ready, are you?'

ALEKSANDRA KASZEWCZUK (16)
St Ronan's College, Lurgan

This Isn't Safe Anymore

I open my eyes, I see everyone. Are they dead? Alive? As I close my eyes I hear whispers, 'We see you, we are coming for you!' Scared, I open my eyes. I'm not safe, I can't escape. If I keep my eyes open I see them. If I close my eyes I hear them. This asylum isn't safe anymore. They are coming to get me. As I try to scream, arms grab and stop me. I try to close my eyes again but these voices... 'This is it, we are coming now!'

CHELSEE MOORE (16)
St Ronan's College, Lurgan

Locked Away

It was a peaceful night, or so I thought as I lay awake on my bed with the moonlight creeping through the window. Strange noises start. The wind started to roar from outside. Fear washed over me. I had a weird urge to look under my bed... I soon gave into it. I was now staring into piercing red eyes; I jumped out of my bed and ran for my door... locked. I turned around and quickly grabbed my keys from the trinket box and inserted it into the lock. I went to turn it but then...

MEGAN GELLATELY (14)
St Ronan's College, Lurgan

Murder House

'C'mon,' shouted Justin, beckoning Freddy into the old, crumbling house. Freddy didn't want to look like a wuss, so he went in. It was cold inside. Suddenly, they heard a loud noise. *Bang!* Justin and Freddy jumped, wondering what the noise was. All of a sudden the front door slammed shut. Then out of nowhere a masked figure appeared and chased the boys. When running, Freddy was faster than Justin and suddenly a door between them closed. Freddy heard Justin scream and then a gunshot. Freddy thought to himself, *Why did I come to this Murder House?*

AIDAN HEANEY (12)
St Ronan's College, Lurgan

The Graveyard

Daylight was leaving. The moon crept out of the clouds. Andy shivered as he walked to his Granny's tomb to place his roses. He thought to himself, *why did it have to be you Granny?* remembering the fatal car accident. The graveyard was engulfed in fog. Andy wanted to leave but got lost. 'I'll call Mum,' said Andy. He called her and she picked up but all Andy could hear was heavy breathing. Andy hung up, an uneasy feeling crept upon him. He waited around with a worried looked staying by the tomb. *Bang!* Dirty hands consumed him.

BRAKLEE IQBAL (11)
St Ronan's College, Lurgan

The Eyes

Tap! Tap! I crawled further under the duvet. *Is the tapping ever going to stop?* I thought to myself. I glanced at the clock. 10.56pm. How can it be? I went to bed at 10.30pm. The tapping got louder and louder. I crawled even further under the duvet. I peeked out through my window. Nothing was there. I blinked. An owl appeared. It just stared at me from the tree outside. I blinked again, it was on the windowsill. 'Mum!' I screamed as loud as I could. The door crept open. Two round eyes stared at me. 'Ahhh!'

AIDAN HUGHES (12)
St Ronan's College, Lurgan

Zombie Invasion

One dark and stormy night, a mad scientist was testing out a potion. His test subject was a wolf cub. After Bob tested it, the wolf had red eyes. He called the wolf Hell Hound. The next day, Bob went to check on Hell Hound but couldn't find him anywhere. Suddenly Hell Hound pinned Bob to the ground and bit him. Bob got really sick and was found dead the next day. His body then went missing before the funeral. Bob was later found.. eating someone. He was a zombie!

BRENDAN AARON AUSTIN (12)
St Ronan's College, Lurgan

The Creeps

In an old rusty cabin deep in the forest, Mr and Mrs Creep lived with no children and nobody nearby. Mr Creep was the biggest and ugliest man in the world. The whole world! As for Mrs Creep, she was the most careless woman in the universe. They always did weird and mischievous things, like prowl around the forest at night wearing overalls. One night the police were patrolling the forest. One officer spotted the pair setting fox and man traps and holding a sniper rifle. The officer went over and asked what they were hunting. They answered, 'You!'...

CONAL MCCANN (11)
St Ronan's College, Lurgan

The Haunted Hospital

The wind grew as I strolled through the naked forest. Nearing the end, there was an abandoned hospital. Anxiously, I wanted to reach home but the fog was down.
With no other choice I approached the hospital. The door was unlocked so I entered; it closed slowly behind me. When I tried opening it again I couldn't...
'Hello?' I said, searching for help. Fortunately there was a torch on the ground, but the batteries? Corroded and out!
I explored the hospital but all I found were remains which was very intimidating.
Suddenly, I felt a *cold* hand around my throat...

FIONTÁN MCCOMB
St Ronan's College, Lurgan

A Walk Down Killing Lane

It was a stormy night and Zack and I were walking down Killing Lane. The rain was beating down and we were drenched but it was only a few more steps to what people called the Spine Chilling House, which was at least somewhere we could take shelter. We pushed open the creaky timber door and entered. *Thud.* The door slammed behind us, Our eyes met for a second in horror and that was when we saw the outline of a shadowy figure wearing a black woollen cloak and a pointed hat. That was the last thing I remember seeing...

JUDE MCCONVILLE (11)
St Ronan's College, Lurgan

Leprechaun

It was a beautiful evening in Ireland. Four teenage students were on holiday. They asked for a ride to a house where people had been killed. A man left a golden watch on a nail outside the house and one by one they died. There were three rocks with symbols on them which acted like a shield. The monster couldn't pass. One girl survived. She ran to the rocks but the monster called more of them to break the shield. They started tearing people apart and chasing the girl through Ireland to take all her gold and terrorise her.

Dylan Ruddy
St Ronan's College, Lurgan

The Animal

One dark and stormy night, four friends had quite a fright. It began when they went into the woods to spend a night if they could. No one knew what was out there and it was not the place to play truth or dare. They all went to sleep without a thought in their heads that in the morning they would all be dead. They could see something through the tent wall, something so terrifying it ended them all. Here's a lesson for all who dare to enter the woods: there's something waiting for you there.

Claire Connolly (14)
St Ronan's College, Lurgan

It's Over!

I walked into the house, the place was in darkness. 'Mum!' I called. No one answered. I slowly walked into the living room. The curtains were blowing like a storm but no windows were open. I slammed the door shut! I swallowed a lump in my throat, headed for the door but it was locked. 'Help!' I screamed, but nobody was there. My heart was racing. Everything went silent.
Then an old, croaky voice sounded all over the house. 'I'm coming for you,' it said. I walked into the kitchen and saw a dark shadowy figure at the window. 'Help!'

TARA BRACKEN (14)
St Ronan's College, Lurgan

The Stranger At The Door

It was a cold winter night and I was in the house on my own. My parents were at the cinema. It was very stormy and there was a lot of thunder. I was watching TV when suddenly it, and all the lights, went out. I was in complete darkness. The house phone wasn't working and there was no power in my mobile. Then I heard someone at the door. It couldn't be my parents. It creaked open and...

CAOIMHE HEANEY
St Ronan's College, Lurgan

Young Writers
Est.1991

YOUNG WRITERS INFORMATION

We hope you have enjoyed reading this book – and that you will continue to in the coming years.

If you're a young writer who enjoys reading and creative writing, or the parent of an enthusiastic poet or story writer, do visit our website www.youngwriters.co.uk. Here you will find free competitions, workshops and games, as well as recommended reads, a poetry glossary and our blog.

If you would like to order further copies of this book, or any of our other titles, then please give us a call or visit **www.youngwriters.co.uk.**

Young Writers
Remus House
Coltsfoot Drive
Peterborough
PE2 9BF
(01733) 890066 / 898110
info@youngwriters.co.uk